Echoes of a Dead Man

When gambler and gunman Matt Lomew arrives in Garner to recuperate from a near-fatal shooting, he isn't looking for trouble. But when his childhood friend Jessie Manners is kidnapped, Matt is forced into an uneasy alliance with the brother of a man he once killed. He knows that such a partnership can only spell trouble but he has nowhere else to turn.

As Matt races to Jessie's rescue, he knows a showdown is inevitable, but he is soon to find out that he is not the only one being haunted by the echoes of a dead man. . . .

Echoes of a Dead Man

Terry James

A Black Horse Western

ROBERT HALE · LONDON

© Terry James 2010
First published in Great Britain 2010

ISBN 978-0-7090-9024-3

Robert Hale Limited
Clerkenwell House
Clerkenwell Green
London EC1R 0HT

www.halebooks.com

Typeset by
Derek Doyle & Associates, Shaw Heath
Printed and bound in Great Britain by
CPI Antony Rowe, Chippenham and Eastbourne

PROLOGUE

'Well, Jethro, you've served your time and paid your debt to society, so keep your nose clean and with luck you and I won't see each other again.' The craggy faced warden, a short man of wide stature and very little hair, pushed back his chair and stood up behind his cluttered desk. 'Here's the watch and the twenty-three dollars you had on you when you were brought in,' he said, handing over a lumpy brown envelope. 'The rest is the stage fare to get you back to Wagoner where you were sentenced.'

Without raising his gaze, Jethro Davies tore the package open and tipped the contents into his hand, glancing disdainfully at the money before shoving it into the pocket of his ill-fitting suit. Like him, the clothing had seen better days and a moth flew out as he withdrew his hand. He watched it flutter towards a ribbon of sunlight coming through a single dirty window, the only brightness in a room made dark by harsh rules, neglect and the same loathing that filled the tiny prison cells beyond its walls.

'Not long now,' the warden said.

Jethro eyed the cracked clock on the wall above the warden's head. It showed eight minutes before midday and he set the watch by it before slipping the timepiece into his vest and returning his gaze to the scarred dirt floor.

Neither man spoke as the clock ticked away the seconds. Maybe the warden had expected a few words of repentance, after all Jethro Davies had been a model prisoner. He had worked hard and stayed out of trouble, paying for his crime with due humility. The warden didn't see many men like that come through his prison. Most were either swallowed into the belly of despair and wasted away, or survived using the same brutality that had brought them to prison in the first place. Jethro had done neither, settling instead into a rare middle ground. And the other men had let him.

The warden had wondered about that in the beginning. After all, the Davies boys were known halfway across the country, their exploits alleged to range from violent robberies to mass murder. Jethro should have been a target for every would-be bad man in the prison, but from the first day he entered, a path had cleared for him. Even Porter, the vicious assistant warden, had resisted the urge to make an example of him.

With a sigh of bewilderment, the old man sat down and made a show of shuffling through a pile of papers while furtively eyeing Jethro. In his late forties, he was a big man at over six feet. He had lost some weight breaking rocks in the hot sun, but the bulk that had added to his formidable presence when he arrived had been replaced with a tautness that reminded the warden of a tightly wound spring ready to explode.

'Mind if I ask you a question?' he asked.

Piercing brown eyes lifted to pin him with an answer, and a shiver hurried along the warden's spine that had nothing to do with the unnatural coolness in the small room. He almost jumped when the clock above his head finally struck twelve. Instead, he broke into a well-practised smile.

'Well, you're a free man, Jethro. I hope you—'

'Save it,' Jethro said, straightening his back and looking him dead in the eye. 'I never met a do-gooder whose words amounted to more than a pile of manure.'

The warden backed away, but before he found any words to say, the door behind Jethro opened and a tall, sinewy man carrying a Colt shotgun across his chest filled the entrance. 'You ready to go, Davies?' he asked.

'What do you think, Porter?' Jethro pushed past, raising his gaze to the sky as he set foot outside the office and breathed deep. Somehow the air that had hung hot and heavy around him for the past four years tasted sweeter today, caressing his face with the tenderness of a high-class whore.

'You want to watch yourself, Jethro,' Porter said behind him. 'It wouldn't take but a word for the warden to get you hauled back in a cell and left to rot.'

'Really? Who'd do it? You?' Jethro said, without any real interest before changing the direction of the conversation. 'I didn't think this was your shift.'

'It isn't. I wanted to see you off.' There was no warmth in the sentiment as he prodded Jethro with the shotgun.

A smile twisted Jethro's lips as Porter herded him forward to where an armed man guarded the gate to freedom. Squinting against the midday sun, Jethro noticed a dust covered rider on a blood bay horse waiting on the outside. As they approached, the rider unhooked his leg from around his saddle pommel and stretched, the movement drawing into sight a black gelding standing riderless alongside.

'Open up,' Porter shouted as they closed in on the guard. 'I've got some trash to put out.'

He laughed at his own joke, but nobody else did as the guard swung the sagging gates open and glanced between Jethro, Porter and the rider outside.

'Miserable son-of-a-bitch,' Porter moaned. 'Go help Freeman with the grub. It sounds like the natives are getting restless.'

The guard looked confused and tipped his head to listen. 'Ain't been this quiet since. . . .'

'I said, go.'

With a shrug, the man wandered away.

'That means you too. Your ride's waiting.'

Porter jabbed the muzzle of the shotgun into Jethro's spine. This time, Jethro pulled up short, fanning his arms wide for balance. He nodded and the rider urged his horse forward.

'Don't start anything, Jethro,' Porter said, stopping short of another prod. 'You might have fooled that milk-sop warden with your meek and mild act but you and I go back a long way and I know you better than that.'

Slowly, Jethro turned to face his antagonist. Above a fixed smile, his eyes held a disturbing twinkle. 'Maybe you used to know me, but times change. I remember eighteen–twenty years back when you, me and Ethan were growing up, how you could have been on the end of the punishment you're handing out nowadays.'

Porter eased his neck inside his dirty collar. 'Yeah, well I ain't, so don't you forget that the next time you back-shoot somebody and end up in this hell-hole.'

Jethro tutted. 'You know that's not my style. How about we shake hands for old time's sake and I get out of here?'

The way Porter looked at Jethro's outstretched hand it could have been a rattler. When he eventually accepted the gesture, he probably wished it was. In one easy motion, Jethro gripped it, pulling Porter forward at the same time turning his own body into him and rolling Porter over his shoulder and flat onto his back in a cloud of dust. By the time Porter realized what was happening, Jethro had his boot pressed against Porter's windpipe and the Colt aimed at his head.

He shifted the muzzle, digging it into Porter's cheek and drawing a trickle of blood. Porter stiffened, but beyond his prison kingdom there was no fight in him, no sign of the bully who ruled his minions with fists and bullets. Jethro pursed his lips as he looked down on his old partner, his expression turning to a smile as a patch of wetness spread across the crotch of Porter's tan pants.

Despite his obvious fear, he sounded surprisingly calm. 'You ain't got any reason to kill me, Jethro. I never crossed you.'

'That's true enough, but you've been keeping something from me, haven't you?'

'How'd you . . ?' Porter's chest heaved as he sucked in what might be his final breath. 'I don't know what's given you that impression.'

Jethro's finger tightened on the trigger.

'All right, maybe I know something that might be of interest to you . . .' Porter's admission petered away, a sudden spark of inspiration flaring before he succumbed completely to his fear. 'But I ain't giving it up without getting something in return.'

Jethro chuckled. 'Are you saying I'll owe you?'

Porter gulped, sweat trickling down his face and diluting the blood on his cheek as it started to crust in the heat beating down on him. 'No, Jethro, you don't owe me anything.' Suddenly, Porter could feel the shadow of death on him. But he hadn't got where he was without a bit of luck and a lot of underhand dealing and he had been saving a special ace for Jethro. 'But what if I could tell you who killed Ethan? Would that be enough to make you just walk away from here and forget you ever saw me?'

The rider dismounted, covering the ground between himself and the two men in a couple of long bounds. He shoved Jethro aside, falling on Porter's chest and gripping him by the throat.

'You know who killed Ethan Davies?'

'Who the hell are you?' Porter asked, struggling as the fight returned to him.

'I'm Stone Davies, and if you know what's good for you, you'll tell me who killed my pa before I slit your throat from ear to ear.'

A Bowie knife seemed to appear out of thin air and Porter looked past the long blade and towards Jethro who stood back with his arms folded across his chest.

'Jethro?' he implored.

'That's what you get for having a big mouth, Porter. I'd tell him what he wants to know, if I were you. He's not as patient as I am. Takes after his pa that way. Once shot a man in the back just for sitting in his chair.'

'I knew it,' Porter said, almost triumphantly. 'Like you said, you'd never shoot a man in the back. You did time for the kid. For Ethan's kid. Jeez, payback's a bitch.'

Jethro shrugged. 'Call it anything you like. It doesn't change the fact that he's got a knife to your throat. Like I said, I'd tell him what he wants to know, if I were you.'

It sounded like good advice as the knife nicked his skin. 'A kid by the name of Bartholomew. That's all they said.'

'Is that his first name? His last name?' Stone asked impatiently.

11

'That's all I know.' He winced as the knife dug deeper. 'A couple of months after it happened, I was banged up in jail overnight sleeping off a hangover. I overheard the circuit judge talking to the sheriff over a couple of glasses of whiskey. He said the kid killed Ethan in self-defence and with what the witness told him it was an open and shut case.'

'Witness?' Stone asked, bringing the knife back into Porter's view. 'We heard Pa was gunned down in an alley and left for dead. No suspects. No witnesses. Are you telling us that was a lie?'

'A cover up maybe. I dunno.' Porter looked into eyes as black and cold as Jethro's. Again the shadow of death touched him as the sun glinted off the evil-looking blade just inches away from his left eye. 'It was a long time ago and I'd had too much to drink, but I think Ethan murdered somebody important. They tried to cover it up. I don't know why. Money I guess. I dunno. I've told you everything I remember.'

Stone shoved the knife into a sheath at the back of his waist and stood up, holding his hand out to Porter. 'You heard any more about this Bartholomew character since?'

Porter stayed where he was and shook his head. 'He disappeared along with the girl who saw what happened. Probably changed his name ... I'm guessing.'

'What about the judge you heard talking, do you remember his name?' Jethro asked, stepping forward with unusual urgency to grab him by the wrist and pull him up.

12

'I think it was Ba . . . Bam . . .' Porter wiped the sweat on his brow as he dug into the recesses of his memory. 'Bamfield. That was it. He retired to Kansas a couple of months back.'

Jethro smiled. 'You did good, Porter. See you around some time.'

Porter sucked in his breath as the Bowie slashed towards him, quickly losing consciousness as blood beaded his shirt across the stomach. Jethro staggered under the dead weight, knocking the knife aside before Stone could finish the job.

'What the hell did you do that for?' Jethro asked, glancing back inside the prison before turning his angry gaze on Stone.

'He ain't no more use to us.'

Jethro shook his head as he lay Porter down, then ripped open his shirt and checked the wound before placing his ear against Porter's chest.

'Is he dead?' Stone asked, hopefully.

'No, it's just a flesh wound. He passed out.'

Using the knife's brass d-ring hang guard, Stone hung it from his finger and offered it to Jethro. 'Finish him off then.'

'You're a stupid son-of-a-bitch. Put it away. Do you think I want to spend any more time in this prison? Do you?' Jethro stood up keeping himself between Stone and Porter. 'Let's get out of here before that guard comes back.'

Stone's eyes narrowed thoughtfully. 'What did he mean about payback?'

'I don't know. Nothing probably.'

'Didn't sound like nothing to me.'

Jethro shoved Stone back towards the horses. 'Look, are we going to stand here talking, or are we going to find the man who killed your pa?'

CHAPTER 1

Five months later

Matt Lomew braced his hand against the door of the Wells Fargo stage, his jangling nerves colliding with his frayed temper as it finally rolled to a stop and he disembarked. He hated travelling by coach, preferred the freedom and fresh air of being on a horse, but although the spirit was willing, the flesh was still weak. Grudgingly, he reached inside the carriage and retrieved a gnarled cane, slipping it under his arm while he waited for his bags to be unloaded.

It was a few minutes before the driver threw down his dusty saddle-bags, and looking around at his new surroundings had improved his mood considerably. Far from being the modest trading post he had left behind a year ago, Garner Creek had grown into a thriving community that at first glance boasted two banks, several classy-looking saloons and a fine-

15

looking hotel aptly named The Grand.

Hefting his bags over his shoulder, he headed for the brightly painted hotel, pulling up short when a rider on a black horse reined up sharply, blocking the way.

'Thought you were dead,' the rider growled.

Matt stood his ground, squinting against a sudden patter of rain as he looked up at the rider, covered in dust, wearing a bandanna across his mouth and a wide brimmed hat pulled low to shadow his face.

'Do I know you?' he asked, tensing as he wondered if maybe this was the man who had put a bullet in his back and left him for dead five months earlier.

'Not yet, but I know all about you.'

The stranger laughed as he eased one leg free of a stirrup and stretched. As his movement momentarily blocked the sky, Matt stiffened under the intense stare of piercing brown eyes. They gave him a mean, sinister look and, as he twisted further in the saddle his coat fell open to reveal a well-handled six-shooter in a scuffed holster.

'Judge Bamford sends his regards,' he said conversationally.

The name set Matt's nerves jangling. There was no reason this stranger should mention it to him. His association with the judge had been short, the reason for it buried along with the man who had made it necessary.

'If you're looking for trouble, I'm not wearing a gun.' Matt flicked the edge of his coat open. 'The sheriff might not look too kindly on you shooting an unarmed man.'

The man on the horse glanced to where a couple of men, including an officious-looking man wearing a badge on his chest, had stopped to watch the exchange. 'You're probably right about that. You best make sure you're tooled up next time we meet.' He spat a line of tobacco at Matt's boots, smiling when minute specks spattered the polished leather.

They glared at each other for what seemed like minutes but was probably only seconds. Suddenly, Matt realized where he had seen that face before, or one very similar. The memory sent a shiver along his spine and he gripped the cane as it provided more support than he had anticipated.

The rider swung his horse away. 'Watch your back, Mr Bartholomew.'

Matt held his breath. Nobody had called him by that name for years. He watched the stranger ride away, his fingers itching to find the .45 buried in his saddle-bag. He didn't believe in ghosts, but he believed in trouble, and that man was trouble with a capital T. Catching sight of the sheriff again, he nodded reverently and continued on to the hotel.

When he entered the lobby, the polished floor squealed under the leather soles of his boots as he paused a moment to appreciate his surroundings. Everything about the place screamed quality and refinement, from the thickly papered walls adorned with paintings of foreign landscapes to the upholstered sofas and glass chandeliers.

17

The man behind the reception desk looked up when he heard the tap-tap of Matt's cane. 'Can I help you, sir?'

'I need a room.'

The man sucked in a whistling breath. 'Sorry, I can't help you, feller. I don't have a room free for the next two weeks. You might try The Beacon. If you go out of here, turn right and it's along on the left.'

Matt studied the man carefully, looking for some hidden motive behind the refusal, but as much as he expected to see one, he couldn't and he decided to try again. 'Are you sure?'

'Even if he's not, I am,' a new voice announced. 'I just showed the last guest to the last available room.'

Both men turned towards the voice and Matt grinned at the look of surprise on the newcomer's face. Closer to forty than fifty, even though his hair was silvery white, his blue eyes held a youthful twinkle that complimented a friendly smile. If Lou Manners resented Matt's unannounced arrival, it didn't show.

'Matt, what the hell are you doing here?' he asked, taking his saddle-bags as he met him halfway across the lobby. 'We thought you were laid up in Silver Springs.'

'I was. I should be according to the doc,' he said, easing himself free of the man's bear hug. 'Besides, I needed to find out what kind of place you're running down here.' He studied his old friend carefully, looking for some sign of disapproval but as much as he expected to see one, he didn't.

'So it's nothing to do with a pretty girl or a big game?'

Both men laughed but Matt couldn't help feeling uneasy. He hadn't come with the intention of playing cards but he couldn't deny the fizz of excitement that stirred in the pit of his stomach. Any other time, his first stop on arriving in town would have been the saloon and an afternoon of poker. As if reminding him why he was really there, a twinge in his back brought him back to reality on a sharp intake of breath.

Lou's brow furrowed with a question but he didn't seem keen to ask it. Instead, he turned to the man behind the desk. 'Dan, I want you to meet Matt Lomew.'

Matt stared into eyes that were now wide with recognition. Dan's heated complexion had paled to a pasty pink, his overbearing confidence draining away with the colour.

'Pleased to meet you, Mr Lomew.'

'It's Matt.'

Dan turned the register around and held out a freshly inked pen. 'If you'll just sign the register.'

It was Lou who took the pen. 'What are you doing, Dan? Matt's family.'

'Oh, of course.' He slapped his forehead, knocking his glasses askew. 'I'll have the room next to yours made ready.'

'Take it easy, Dan,' Lou warned him. 'I told you, Matt is family. Whatever you've heard, forget it.'

Dan nodded but the reassurance apparently did little to settle his nerves as he fumbled to straighten his spectacles before spinning on his heel. His brisk exit didn't exactly surprise Matt; after all it was a reaction he had grown accustomed to, even if he hoped for something else.

'Lou, can we talk?' Matt stumbled as he adjusted his stance, the cane wobbling as it took more of his weight.

'You been drinking?'

He hated the sympathetic way Lou looked him over but he guessed it was something he was going to have to get used to if he decided to stay. 'No. I had to give it up,' he said, lightly.

'I can see why. What's on your mind?'

Matt took a deep breath. 'Jessie. How is she?'

Lou shrugged, seemingly unwilling to comment. 'She's glad you're still alive, still mad as hell that you didn't let us know what happened sooner.'

'I wanted to make sure I was going to walk again before I let her start fussing.'

'You don't need to explain yourself to me.' Lou lifted Matt's chin, his blue eyes full of concern. 'You look tired. Why don't you rest up, give yourself time to think of a way to make it up to her?'

Matt nodded. 'I don't want to cause trouble, Lou.'

'It never stopped you before.' There was no malice. 'That frown you're wearing tells me it isn't going to stop you now. What's wrong?'

'I just ran into a dead man.'

'What the hell's that supposed to mean?'

Matt's gaze circled the lobby, his expression serious as he stepped in closer. 'I just ran into a man who's a dead ringer for Ethan Davies.'

CHAPTER 2

Matt didn't flinch when he heard the door ease open behind him, but it wasn't fear or surprise that held him still. It was just that he never made a move until he knew exactly what he was facing. By his reckoning, too many men in the West had died because of a misunderstanding and he wasn't prepared to add to their number. Besides, his visitor hesitated on the threshold, no doubt considering what move to make next, so Matt had time on his side. With practised patience, he waited, continuing to study the scene beyond his window.

His interest was immediately drawn to one gent in particular among the dozens of unknown faces. Of average height, wearing a red shirt and black pants, and a sombrero that shaded his face, nothing about him was particularly unusual. The only reason Matt had noticed him was because he had been there, silent and unmoving among a thronging mass, for almost an hour. Whether he was watching the hotel or the road was hard to say, since his standpoint offered an excellent view of both and his gaze never lingered on any particular place. But if Matt had to put money on it, he would say the man was watching the hotel.

'Are you enjoying the view, Jessie?' Matt's eyes swept around, fixing the pretty blonde with a glint of amusement.

She let out her breath, breaking into an impish grin as she leaned against the back of the door, closing it fully. 'How do you always know I'm there? It makes n—' Her smile faded as her gaze moved across his torso.

He had stopped noticing the fresh scars where three bullets had torn through his flesh in quick succession, but the look of disgust on her face showed they were as ugly as he remembered them. Quickly, he turned his attention to dressing. Already wearing black pants, he slipped on a crisp white shirt before hesitating over a fancy vest, his hand changing direction to find the gun-belt hanging beside it on the bedstead. As if it were a part of him, he buckled it around his hips before tying the holster to his thigh.

'So, how do you always know I'm there?' she asked, a forced lightness in her voice.

'You're predictable.'

A narrow-eyed glance in her direction threatened to contradict him. In the months since he had last seen her, Jessie had blossomed from a girl into a woman. The blue cotton dress she wore, slightly pinched at the waist, couldn't disguise the fuller figure underneath. And as for her hair, bunched at the back and tied with a red ribbon, it lent her an elegance he didn't recognize. She about took his breath away. The only link with reality was the girlish shine in her eyes and the high colour of her sun-kissed cheeks, which gladly betrayed her youth.

Straightening up, he slipped on the vest, fastening each button before sliding the silver handled, custom-made .45 out of its holster. He'd practised the action a thousand times but it never lost its appeal, especially when she was there.

She sauntered across to meet him, stopping close enough to reach up and smooth back a lock of damp hair. 'Predictable? Then why did you just look at me as if you never saw me in a dress before?'

He shrugged, still shaken by the unexpected sight she presented. 'You've changed while I've been away.'

She turned away to the cheval mirror pushed into the corner. After smoothing her dress and plumping her hair, she faced him through the glass.

'Yes, I have.' Her tone was gentler. 'I'm not a girl anymore: I'm a woman.'

She searched the reflection of his face in the glass, but he knew all she saw was the passive mask of a gambler. Even his eyes, which could be hazel or black depending on his mood, gave nothing away as his steady gaze met hers in the mirror.

'Damn it! I could hate you sometimes.' She took a deep breath, settling herself and adopting a gentler tone. 'But I don't, so be nice to me. Today's my birthday. I'm eighteen. You don't have to treat me like a kid anymore.'

'Eighteen? I can just about remember when I was that young,' he mumbled, preferring not to conjure the image. 'Seems like a long time ago.'

She spluttered on a derisive laugh. 'You'd like to think so. It's true you're twenty-two going on forty-two but don't forget one thing: I've known you for a long time and deep down you're a kid just like me.'

She cocked her head, daring him to deny it, but he refused to start an argument he couldn't win.

'All right.' She held up her hands in mock surrender. 'It's my birthday and I'm not arguing with you. Only, just this once, try to see me as more than a snot-nosed kid, will you?'

Turning suddenly, she collided with him, tilting her head to look up at him, thereby offering a view of her cleavage. It was tempting, all that flesh pressed right up against him. But she deserved better than that, and even if she didn't know it, he did.

'Lou told me you're here to stay this time. Does that mean I can start making plans for us now?'

The suggestion wrong-footed him and he frowned. It seemed to amuse her, but more than that, it impassioned her with a fire he hadn't expected. Stepping away from him, she fixed her hair again as she watched him through the mirror.

'Know this, Matt Lomew, I've got a passionate heart and a head full of dreams, but I'm no fool. Now I've got you here, I don't intend to let you slip through my fingers again.'

Her newfound confidence surprised him, but he

25

was seeing her in a whole new light and he liked what he saw. Just how far she'd go to get what she wanted he didn't know, but it was going to be fun finding out.

'I'm not one of your awkward farm boys, Jess. Be careful where you're going with this.'

She chuckled. 'I know what you are, Matt. You're a gambler, a gunman and a drifter.'

The facts sobered him, reminded him of the cold hard truth and the look on her face a few minutes before. 'That's right. Not the marrying kind.'

She picked his hat up off the dresser and handed it to him before opening the door. 'No, but you're a betting man and I'm willing to bet I can change your mind.'

Her unbending certainty was starting to make him doubt his own mind and he grabbed her hand, deciding to leave his cane behind as she grasped her fingers tightly through his. 'Come on,' he said, 'let's take a stroll and show off that pretty dress before I have to show you what kind of trouble a promise like that can get you into.'

CHAPTER 3

Along Main Street, the setting sun cast long shadows made eerie by a chill breeze and an unusual stillness. As if she felt it too, Jessie linked her arm through Matt's, clutching her breast to his elbow as they walked. It took more bluff than a pair of twos for him not to pull away, but the general store offered some respite and he bolted for it leaving Jessie to enjoy the admiring glances of passers-by.

When he emerged a few minutes later, he was clutching a box of candy wrapped in paper and tied with a ribbon. He stopped dead, not sure what was wrong until he realized he was alone. Looking left and right, across the street towards the dress shop, he couldn't find Jessie. He checked outside the barbershop and bathhouse, the mercantile, a cheap hotel and the sheriff's office, the length and breadth of the rutted street and back again. She was nowhere obvious. Then, just as he was about to head for the hotel, he glimpsed her standing outside the Grand Piano saloon, her head tipped quizzically to one side as she listened. Coming from behind closed doors

27

and through an open window, the chords of a piano accompanied a high singing voice, glasses clinked and voices clashed in a cacophony of sound.

She looked his way and pointed inside. 'I want to go in there,' she mouthed across the suddenly busy street.

That might well be, but even outside a saloon was no place for a decent girl to be and he shook his head.

'Please,' she whined silently.

He shook his head emphatically, motioning with his finger for her to join him before turning back towards the hotel. When he glanced over his shoulder, expecting to find Jessie on her way, he didn't like what he saw. The stranger in the red shirt, who had been watching the hotel, had stopped to talk to her as he tied his horse to a hitch-rail. On closer inspection, Matt recognized the type. A cowpuncher, washed and shaved and wearing a shirt that still had store-bought creases, in town for the weekend, looking for a good time.

Predictably, he touched the brim of his sombrero and Jessie smiled, blushing slightly as she lowered her lashes shyly. Matt's gut tightened with foreboding. On Jess, it was downright sweet and far too appealing for a cowboy with a pocketful of money and his pants full of ideas. As Matt knew he would, the man swept off his hat and vaulted over a water trough to join her.

'You don't want to do this,' a man's voice whispered from behind him. 'It's too soon. Just walk away. Live to fight another day.'

It sounded like a threat; it could have been a warning. Matt didn't know or care. Spinning around, he saw only the top of a hat belonging to a big, lean individual dressed in tan shirt and pants with his arms folded across his chest. Despite the familiar-looking Smith & Wesson holstered low on his hip, he seemed more intent on studying his dusty boots than getting involved. Shoving the candy at him, Matt bounced into the road, feeling his joints creak as he landed awkwardly in sun-dried wheel ruts. He sensed the man move behind him as he pulled up short, waiting impatiently for a laden wagon to pass.

Starting towards Jessie again, he dodged a horse and rider, all the while keeping his focus on the scene unfolding twenty feet in front of him. Jessie obviously realized the danger. She tried to duck sideways but the man's arm blocked her as he leaned in close to whisper against her ear. The wide-eyed look of uncertainty, of being out of her depth, was unmistakable. She placed her hand on his chest, trying to shove him away while at the same time she retreated until her back met the wall.

Matt broke into a stilted sprint. The blood ran cold through his veins, freezing his emotions and heightening his resolve. He didn't know the man, didn't need to or want to. But if he hurt Jess, he'd see him in hell.

'Sir, please, let me pass.' Jessie's politeness sounded laughable under the circumstances. 'You've made a mistake.'

'You mean because I'm new in town and we haven't been properly introduced? Well, hell, that ain't a problem.' His fingers stroked up and down her neck. 'My name's Stone Davies. Now if you tell me your name we're as good as old friends.'

She knocked his hand away and pressed closer to the wall. Still he teased her, leaving no room for escape as he reached into his pocket and pulled out a couple of bills. Placing his lips close to her ear, he shoved the money into the front of her dress.

'Don't do that,' she said.

'Aw, come on. You know you were standing here just waiting for me.' He gripped her elbow, dragging her towards the saloon doors. 'Don't play games with me now. Let's go inside and get properly acquainted over a drink and then later. . . .'

Matt lunged, grabbing him by the arm and spinning him like a top so that he had no choice but to sprawl in the dirt. By the time he found his feet, Matt had already taken in the once broken nose and white scars that detailed his face and marked him as a brawler. The way he carried his gun seemed to back that up, being tied a little too low against his thigh, probably more for show than effect.

'You! I thought you were dead.'

Matt registered the name, Stone Davies, as he tried to match it with the face. In his line of work, he met a lot of men but this one chilled him to the core. For the second time in as many days, he was staring at the face of a ghost. As naturally as breathing, his hand moved to rest on his belt buckle.

'Are you the son-of-a-bitch who put a bullet in my back?' he asked, calmly.

Davies grinned. 'I am if you're the son-of-a-bitch who killed my pa.'

Stone snatched for his gun almost before he had finished talking, but a bullet nicking his ear shocked him into stillness before he drew it fully. For a moment, he gawped as if he couldn't believe what had happened. Staring down the barrel of a gun that had apparently appeared out of thin air, the fight gushed out of him as quick as the colour from his freckled cheeks.

Gingerly checking his bloody ear was still intact, he sounded almost appreciative. 'Damn, you're fast.'

'Yes, I am.' Matt holstered his gun. 'So, what happens now? Are you going to wait for me to turn my back like last time?'

Around them, people scattered. Inside the saloon, faces pressed against dirty windows. Sudden and absolute silence shrouded the evening with deadly anticipation. Stone's mouth almost twitched into a smile as he matched Matt's unwavering stare.

'I don't need to,' he said, fanning his arm wide as if in introduction.

Slow footsteps marked the arrival of a man who, even without the black horse under him, was a fearful sight. He walked like a king moving among his subjects, unhurried, head high, back straight. A big man in a small town, good enough with the Smith & Wesson he carried to keep all-comers at bay. Anybody with an interest could see at a glance that the tan-clad stranger didn't fit the role of rancher or businessman. He was too watchful, taking in every detail without appearing to notice anything in particular.

When he finally stopped beside Stone and looked into Matt's eyes, there was none of the doubt Matt expected to see. This man wasn't pretending to be somebody important, he believed he was. And yet, despite his arrogance, when he was less than four feet away, he stopped, his thin mouth widening into a caricature of a smile.

'I guess this time I'll introduce myself. Name's Jethro Davies.' His speech was unhurried and he held out his hand in an easy greeting. 'Mind if I call you Matt?'

Matt kept his arms at his sides, taking nothing for granted, refusing to be ruffled by the friendly informality.

'Or would you prefer Bartholomew on your cross?' Stone's tone seethed contempt.

Matt slowed his breathing, forcing himself to be calm as the upcoming scene played in his mind like a recurring nightmare. First the stare down, then the tension building between them and finally the draw. Only this time, something was different. The tension was already building in Matt but he couldn't see it in Jethro's glassy stare.

He hoped Jethro Davies couldn't see it in his.

Suddenly, Matt remembered Jess. If his instinct was right, she shouldn't see what happened next. 'Jessie, go back to the hotel.' He choked out the

32

words, struggling against a throat gone dry as bark.

Stone spat in the dirt. 'She stays. She's already bought and paid for and I'm going to make sure I collect on every penny. Are you just going to stand there, Jethro, or are you going to settle this?'

Matt tensed but neither he nor Jethro reacted. A wrong move by either of them might result in death for both at such close quarters and whatever else Jethro had in mind wouldn't include getting killed.

That didn't seem to occur to Jessie as she moved in behind Matt and flung the bills back at Stone. 'I'm not for sale. You can take your money.'

'That ain't the way it works around here, pretty. You offered the goods, I paid for them. There's no going back because you see some Fancy Dan you like the look of better 'n me.' His glare fixed on Matt with a telltale flicker of resentment. 'If you don't want to see this kid's guts splattered in the dirt, you just scoot your butt over here and get ready to finish what we started.'

The words were more for Matt than Jessie, an attempt to rile him into making a mistake that would give either Stone or Jethro, or maybe both, a chance to kill him in an unguarded moment.

'I didn't start anything,' Jessie said, her indignation tangible. 'But you lay one finger on me and it'll be your guts splattered in the dirt, mister.'

'That'll do, Jessie,' Matt said, her words piling more weight on his gun hand than he needed. 'You made your point.'

Surprisingly, Jethro agreed. 'And you hush up too,

Stone, or that mouth of yours is going to get you killed.' Jethro's calm seemed to falter. 'Go get yourself a drink. I'm sure there are plenty of other girls who'll be happy to spend time with you.'

'Do you think I'm scared of a kid with a gun?' Stone yelled. ' 'Cause I ain't.'

'That's because, boy, God didn't give you the sense of a piece of wood. You already proved that once. Next time you might lose more than the tip of an ear. Go inside and have a drink. Let me handle this.'

A gasp rippled through the crowd as those gawkers nearest the front, edged back. Although Stone looked ready to blow, his jaw twitched as he bit down on whatever he wanted to say and glared into a face older but undeniably a mirror image of his own. Despite Jethro's affable smirk, the animosity crackled between them. Whatever Stone expected, the older man apparently revelled in disappointing him.

A tense few seconds passed before Stone finally spat in the dirt and announced, 'This ain't over.' Without a glance in any direction, he shouldered past Matt and stamped into the saloon, the doors banging long after he yelled for whiskey.

Jethro watched him go, his eyes narrowed, but when he turned his attention back to Matt only amusement showed. 'I'd like to apologize for my nephew, but I won't. He's got his reasons for wanting you dead.' He tossed another hard glance in the direction of the saloon. 'Suppose I should have too, seeing as how you killed my brother, but time gives a man plenty of time to think and a pretty girl can give him a hundred reasons not to want to die.' He turned his strange stare on Jessie. 'Tell me something, girl, was your mother's name Marianne?'

She didn't answer.

Jethro chuckled. 'I don't need your answer to know I'm right. You look just like her when she was your age.' He dismissed her, his odd gaze returning to Matt. 'She changes things a mite, raises the stakes higher than revenge.'

Matt's fingers itched to draw his .45. 'Leave her out of this.'

'Or what? You'll kill me?'

Jethro stepped in quickly, two long paces bringing him within striking distance. The unexpected advance caught Matt off-guard and, as he stepped backwards, he collided with Jessie, losing his already tenuous balance. It was all the time Jethro needed and he rammed his fist into Matt's stomach doubling him over before clenching his hands in a single fist that smashed down hard on Matt's back and slammed him into the dirt. A final kick in the chest was enough to keep him down, gasping for air.

Jessie threw herself between them. 'Leave him alone. He's had enough.'

Matt tried to shove her aside, but she clung to him, shielding him with her body despite Jethro's raised fist. In a fleeting moment, something seemed to register on Jethro's face. Surprise? It was hard to tell, but as quickly as he had attacked, he turned on his heel and followed Stone's tracks to the saloon.

Before he went inside, he hesitated without

looking back. 'Ain't any doubt in my mind now, Jessica-Rose, that you're Marianne's daughter. She was a fighter too, although she didn't realize it.'

'Nobody calls me that. How do you know that's my name?'

He laughed. 'Tell me, do you love him?'

The question was completely unexpected but Jess didn't waste a heartbeat thinking about her answer. 'I do.'

'Then don't give up without a fight, will you?'

He pushed inside, and seconds later, someone started playing the piano. Outside on the street, folks moved about their business, some disappointed at the outcome, others relieved. Without the blood and gore of a gunfight, life carried on as before.

But things had changed. Matt felt it in the chill breeze that tickled his neck as he let Jessie help him to his feet. This wasn't a minor disagreement, some sore loser looking to take back the pot, or even simple revenge. Jethro wanted Matt to know he would take his life and his girl, and probably not in that order. More worrying was the knowledge that for the first time in a long time Matt wasn't sure he could stop him.

Jessie ducked under his arm, steadying him as he rocked on his feet. 'Matt, what are you going to do?'

He faltered, grabbing his leg above the knee as it threatened to give way. *Damn it.* He had thought a couple of day's rest would be enough, but the weakness was still with him, and Jethro's unexpected beating hadn't helped. He wrapped his arm around

Jessie's shoulders, avoiding her tide of questions as he limped to the hotel. What could he say anyway? That all he wanted to do was throw her on a horse, mount up and ride away someplace where no one would find them?

Was that what he wanted, to run for the rest of his life?

CHAPTER 4

Heads turned as they crossed the street, the faces showing a mixture of sympathy and contempt. Nothing that had happened had been his fault, but that didn't make him less responsible in the minds of the townsfolk. All they saw was the gun and the fancy clothes. Their imaginations filled in the rest, including God only knew what filthy notions about him and Jessie. Just the idea of it bothered him. He had never thought about anything except keeping her safe, but now he realized there was more to it than finding her a home and being a friend.

Matt doubted Jessie even noticed. When they reached the hotel, a quick assurance to Lou that he would explain everything later was all he could manage before she dragged him upstairs to his room. When she sat beside him on the bed, her tight-lipped silence worried him more than the prospect of a showdown with Jethro Davies. Despite the weakness in his legs, he left her and went to look out of the window.

'That was a foolish thing you did, mouthing off at

Stone Davies and then throwing yourself between Jethro and me. You could have been hurt.' More than ever he believed that he wasn't the marrying kind and he steeled himself against sentimentality. 'It can't happen again.'

'I'm sorry. I couldn't just stand there and—'

'I know and that's why it's not safe for you to be around me. I'm going to ask Lou to send you away for a while.'

'I won't go.'

'You won't go?' he asked, genuinely surprised that she would argue with him.

'No. I'm as safe here as I am anywhere. You'll protect me like you always have.'

'Things are different. These men, they've waited a long time to catch up with me.'

'Do you think I don't know that?'

Did she? Had she somehow made the connection between Stone and Jethro and the man who murdered her grandfather? No. She believed that man had been a nameless drifter. Matt couldn't bring himself to ask the question. She never talked about what happened and her nightmares had all but stopped the past couple of years. He wouldn't do anything to rekindle them now.

'The fact is, being around me's dangerous and whatever happens to me, I don't want you getting hurt.'

'I know that, but we've been in trouble before, like that night you found me when my grandpa was killed.'

'This time it's different.'

'So you keep saying. And I'll say it again: do you think I don't know that? That it makes a difference to me?'

Matt had never realized it before, but given the chance, she would walk beside him no matter what. And she could be unnervingly quick and quiet when she chose to be. Spinning around to face her, he reeled as she wrapped her arms around him, the lilac scent in her hair offering a secondary attack he hadn't been expecting.

'Stop it, Jessie. You won't change my mind. I want you gone from here in the morning.'

Tears welled in her eyes but there was no surrender. 'You don't have to fight them. You could leave with me.'

He shook his head and turned his back on her, but she grabbed his arm, refusing to let his stubborn silence deter her. 'Let go of the past, Matt. Ethan Davies is dead, but we're still alive.'

That rocked him. The truth weighed him down physically and mentally and allowed his mind to snap back to a night he had tried to forget. It had been a while since he had thought about it. Ethan Davies had gone to Jessie's home, thirsty for blood. An evil man who tortured and murdered, leaving nothing and no one untouched. The images were still clear, even if the pain had dulled. In his mind's eye, Matt could still see her grandpa dying on the floor in a pool of blood. He remembered the fear that had turned her to stone when the devil with the red hair

40

and the piercing eyes had found her hiding behind a chair.

She had cowered like a dog, begging him not to hurt her. Beyond the image of terror and pain, he could still see the hope that the sight of him had given her. That's when Matt had done the first decent thing of his whole short life. Just a skinny kid with barely a whisker on his chin, holding a gun in his hand that wobbled, he had stepped out of the shadows.

'Let her go, you son-of-a-bitch.'

His voice had been loud and sharp, full of fear, not fully a man's, but the gun never left its target. As Ethan turned around, snatching for his gun, Matt fired and threw himself to the side the way he had seen gunfighters do. Ethan tried to fire as he staggered backwards, but already blood soaked his stomach, the pain doubling him over. For several seconds, he didn't move. Pain or shock rendered him speechless. His eyes widened, then rolled. Like a giant oak, he tumbled, getting off a single shot that nicked Matt's thigh, throwing him further off balance as he fumbled the hammer and squeezed the trigger again and again. . . .

The present returned with a warm hand on his cheek. Slowly, familiar features merged into focus. The sights and sounds of a past best forgotten, cleared from his mind. Looking about, he welcomed the familiarity of everything around him from the freshly papered walls to the polished wooden floor, the bed, the dresser and finally the long mirror that

41

mocked him with its stark reflection of a foolish boy.

'Did you hear what I said?' Jess asked, shaking him slightly. 'Let's forget Stone and Jethro and just run like we did before.'

As much as he had toyed with that idea on the way back to the hotel, he knew it couldn't happen. All it proved was how much she loved him, what she would do to be with him. It was woman's thinking, a final attempt to reason with his heart instead of his head.

'You heard what they said. They want me dead and God only knows what they'd do to you. Wherever we go they might find us.' He turned again to the window, twitching the curtain to see out into the darkening street. 'It's time to stop running and put an end to the past for good.'

'Then let me help you. I brought this trouble down on you and I should share some of the responsibility for ending it.'

He looked at her sideways, wondering which trouble she meant, past or present. As always he discarded his memories of the past and planted himself firmly in the present. 'I killed his brother and he wants revenge for that. What happened today has nothing to do with that outcome. All it proved is that it's time for you to forget your ideas about me and get on with your own life, a new life without me in it.'

'I don't want a new life. I want the life I have *with* you in it. Why are you already talking like a dead man? Do you think getting yourself killed is going to save me?' Unexpectedly, she thumped him on the back, drawing an involuntary gasp as a spasm of pain

42

coursed along his spine and sent pins and needles racing along his leg. 'Quit talking to me like I'm a child, Matt, and look at yourself. You're not well yet. You've lost weight, you can barely stand without something to lean on, and you look like you haven't slept in a month. You're the one who's not thinking straight.'

Running a hand through his hair was something he did when he was nervous and he hated himself as he did it now and turned to face her. Even so, a chuckle curved his mouth into a half smile. She had given him an advantage and he was about to use it.

'You're right. I'm not the man I was, but it's got nothing to do with the bullet lodged in my back or the lack of a good night's sleep. It's you. When I'm near you, I can't think straight. You twist me around until I don't know which direction I'm facing. Do you think Jethro Davies is going to care about any of that when he calls me out to kill me?'

Their argument had reached a crescendo and now it crashed around them and lay in ruins. They stood a couple of feet apart and yet a hundred miles might as well have separated them. Matt had played his hand and gone all-in, knowing she wouldn't bet against his life, but there was no satisfaction in the win as a grim chuckle admitted her defeat.

'You're a shrewd gambler, Matt. I should have known I'd never win against you in a fair fight. But this isn't a fair fight because there's something you don't know that might just save your life.'

He raised a curious eyebrow despite his

determination not to fuel her argument.

'Do you know how he knew my mother's name? How he knew mine?'

Matt hadn't given it much thought and he didn't now. 'It doesn't matter.'

'It does, because it means we have something to bargain with.'

'There's no bargaining with men like Jethro Davies.'

A knock at the door silenced any argument she might have offered.

'Matt. They're calling for you over at the Nugget.' It was Lou. 'The game starts in ten minutes, with or without you. My five thousand dollars says it'd be better with.'

'Surely you aren't going after what happened,' she whispered, worry once again replacing the anger that had slowly replaced it. 'You need to see the doctor.'

He shook his head and whispered, 'I can't let Lou down.' Then shouted, 'I'll be there.'

'Good boy. I'm counting on you to win me some money. And another thing: if you keep my ward in there any longer, there'll be a shotgun waiting for you when you come out.'

As Lou's footsteps faded, Matt straightened his vest and reached for his coat. Jessie took it from him, holding it while he slipped into it, then refusing to let go until he faced her.

'I know you mean well, Jessie, but you need to stay out of this. What happened in the past was my doing.' He wiped a tear from her cheek. 'And if I had

44

it to do again, I would. We both know the way it is between us, the way it's always been, but what good's the truth now?'

She reached up and smoothed back an unruly lock of his hair. For the first time in a long time, he didn't squirm under her scrutiny. Hesitantly, she traced his profile with her fingertips, as if memorizing the roughness of his cheek, his straight nose, the slight cleft in his chin and finally the narrow line of his lips.

Her hand trembled, mimicking the pleasure and pain that suddenly churned his insides. He hated to see her anguish and know he was the cause of it, but it wasn't in him to give her false hope. Crushed by her emotions, she wrapped her arms around his waist and hugged him, her heart full of hurt she didn't want to hide, but he couldn't reciprocate and he pushed her to arm's length, keeping his voice low and steady.

'I know you don't understand, Jess. You believe in heroes and happy-ever-afters but you deserve more than I can give you. You know that, don't you?'

She shook her head stubbornly, but there were no tears now. Only ice showed in the blue depths of her eyes, a coldness he had never seen before, and didn't like. It inclined him to say more than he intended.

'Listen to me. You said it yourself. I'm a drifter. A gambler. A gunman. I go where the wind takes me. I always play the hand I'm dealt . . . and one day I'll meet somebody who shoots better than I do. Maybe today I already did.'

'I know all that.' Her tone was as cold as the ice behind her eyes.

'Then stop fighting me.'

She brushed his coat where tears had formed a damp patch on his shoulder, then shoved him towards the door. Pulling it open, she pushed him into the hallway. 'Don't ask me to give up my dreams, Matt. I can't do that, even for you. You go and play the hand you're dealt, and I'll play mine, maybe somehow we'll end up in the same game.'

CHAPTER 5

Jessie didn't feel much like talking to anyone after Matt left. Certainly she couldn't face Lou after what had happened outside the saloon. Grudgingly she admitted that Matt was right about one thing: she shouldn't have been there. She had let herself and Lou down, standing there like a floozy outside a place like that. But she had wanted Matt to notice her, to prove to him that she was ready to join him in his world. All she had proved was that she had no idea what living in his world really meant. She wasn't even sure she could after the way he drew iron on Stone Davies. That was the first time since Ethan Davies's death that she'd seen him draw his gun in anger. She hoped it was the last, but somehow she doubted it.

Stepping away from the open window where the night had started to draw a veil over the street below, she looked around Matt's room. For the first time, she really saw it and realized it was like any other in the hotel. There was nothing in it to show who it belonged to. Not even a small memento or

47

photograph placed fondly on the table beside the bed. Absentmindedly she opened the dresser drawers and the narrow armoire. Empty. Maybe she had been lying to herself all along. He had never intended to stay for her, and yet he refused to leave now that his life depended on it.

Feeling suddenly over-tired and irritable, she started to pace. 'Damn you, Matt Lomew,' she said aloud. 'Why did you save me just to let me die a little every day?'

As she passed the window something caught her attention. An unexpected sound. The creak of a weathered board bending under an unexpected weight? Trying to act as though nothing was amiss, she continued to pace, drawing to a natural stop beside the window where she pressed herself tight against the wall to listen.

'Jessica-Rose?'

She swallowed a burst of fear that set her heart racing and the blood to pounding loudly in her ears as she recognized the voice. But there was an element of excitement too, of curiosity, and maybe hope. How did he know her name? Had he really known her mother? Maybe he had even known her father. The questions racing around her head far outweighed the panic that shifted the weight to her toes and left her tight as a wound spring ready to explode into action at the slightest inclination.

'I know you're in there. I saw you watching the street.' Jethro Davies poked his head inside, his gaze circling the room before finding her frozen against the wall. He smiled. 'You might not believe this, but you don't need to be afraid of me: I haven't come to hurt you.'

Before she could run past, he kicked his legs over the sill, but instead of coming fully into the room, he perched on the ledge with his hands planted comfortably on his knees. For a few seconds, he didn't say anything as he looked her over from the top of her head to the tip of her toes before settling on her face. There was something almost affectionate in the small smile that curved his lips. Even his odd gaze seemed to soften as he looked at her.

'What do you want?' she asked, trying to control the tremor in her voice. 'Matt will be back any time now.'

He chuckled. 'He left for the game ten minutes ago and he won't be back for hours. But there's no need for you to worry, I only stopped by for a moment.'

She hesitated over the obvious question, afraid to break the thrill of curiosity coursing through her veins, but she had to ask. 'Why? Why did you come?'

'I wanted to be sure of something.'

Again she hesitated. 'What?'

'That you're really Marianne's daughter.'

Just the mention of her mother's name brought a lump to her throat, but the opportunity to talk to someone who had known her stopped the sadness from overwhelming her. 'My mother's name was Marianne,' she said, barely able to contain her

49

curiosity. 'Did you know her?'

He nodded.

'And my father?'

This time it was his turn to hesitate. 'I knew them both. Your mother was a fine and good woman.'

'And my father?'

'He was a good man. Do you remember him at all?'

She nodded, recalling his soft laughter and the gentleness of his big hands. 'A little. Playing games mostly. I was very small when he died. It's hard to remember the details.'

'He loved playing games with you. You made him laugh a lot. You and your mother. He was very happy back then before. . . .'

She held her breath, waiting, eager for whatever details he might provide. When he didn't continue, she prompted, 'Before what?'

'Before your mother died.' The light disappeared from his eyes, his expression turning as grey and cold as rock. He stood abruptly, turning on a dime and gripping her shoulders in a painful hold. 'Listen to me. If you don't want the same life as your parents, you need to talk to Matt, convince him that he can't win this fight.'

His certainty irked her. 'Why? Because you gave him a beating today? In a fair fight, he's as fast as any man with a gun. Or maybe you're the one who's afraid.'

He shook her roughly, letting go suddenly as though she were a hot coal. 'Listen to me, Jessica-

Rose. Your mother had the same unflinching belief in your pa that you have in Matt, but when trouble came, it didn't come head on. It snuck up on them from behind and there was nothing your pa could do to stop it. Your ma died because your pa thought he could reason with trouble, or win against it in a fair fight. Well it wasn't a fair fight then and it won't be now. Stone'll come from behind, in the dead of night, and next time Matt won't be as lucky as he was in Silver Springs.'

She knew he was telling the truth about Matt's luck. Even Lou, who never commented on Matt's way of life, had admitted that no man should have lived after being riddled with four bullets. And after their showdown this afternoon, there was no doubt Stone had been the man behind them. But why should Jethro care?

'If you're not afraid of going up against Matt, why are you bothering to warn me? Surely your loyalty lies with your nephew.'

His look of indecision only added to her determination to find out what game he was playing.

'What aren't you telling me?'

When he didn't answer, she stamped to the door, intending to throw it wide and order him out but he followed quickly, shaking the panels as he slammed his palm against them before she could fully open it.

'Because earlier today, you told me you loved him,' he said, raising his voice above its even pitch for the first time, 'and I saw the same unwavering certainty in your eyes as I did in your mother's.

Believe me when I tell you, I don't want to kill him, but nothing I can say is going to stop Stone from trying. And whatever else happens, I owe it to your mother to make sure you don't get caught up in the middle of it.'

His mixture of concern and veiled threats was confusing to say the least and with everything else falling to pieces around her, she was in no mood for riddles. 'Stop talking about my mother. I'm starting to wonder whether you even knew her or my father. If you did, you'd know she died in a tragic accident and my father . . . he died of a broken heart. As for Matt and me, we faced the Devil together once before, we can do it again. Maybe you're the one who should think about leaving.'

'You're warning me to get out of town?' He chuckled and stepped away, still laughing as he headed for the window. 'You really are your mother's daughter, Jessica-Rose,' he said, swinging his legs over the sill and out onto the narrow porch that ran the length of the hotel. 'But you're a day-dreamer like your father. Just for the record, nobody ever died of a broken heart. You might want to think about that.'

And with that he was gone.

CHAPTER 6

Four players had already taken their seats when Matt entered the private gaming room of the Big Nugget Saloon. He recognized Hank McCreedy, a cattleman known for more than 200 miles as Smiling Hank. True to his reputation, he eyed Matt with something akin to amusement, then smiled and waved him to a seat opposite. Beside the amply proportioned cattleman sat Carl Langton, owner of the local bank and a favourite with the ladies despite his advancing years. The other two men Matt didn't recognize but he guessed they were locals by the easy way they were chatting between themselves.

'Looks like we might have two empty seats tonight, gentleman,' Hank McCreedy said after a few minutes. Leaning back in his chair, he checked his gold pocket watch. 'I make it almost nine.'

Langton looked at his own timepiece, pressed it to his ear and tapped the glass before checking it again. 'I would agree, Hank. Will we wait?'

McCreedy shifted his gaze and nodded to a suited, balding man leaning idly by the door. 'Don't like tardiness in my business dealings. Don't see why I should allow it at my table.'

The doorman straightened officiously, but before he could turn the brass key, the door swung open.

'Evening, gents.' Jethro Davies handed a wedge of money to the man at the door and nodded to each of the players before letting his gaze meet and hold Matt's.

Behind him, Stone pushed to get in. 'Are we in time?'

McCreedy glanced slyly in Matt's direction then looked at his watch as if it was the first time. 'Take a seat. We were just about to get started.'

Occupying the chair to McCreedy's left, Jethro leaned aside as the doorman placed a pile of chips in front of him. 'Matt, it's good to see you. I hear you're good with a deck of cards.'

Matt took a sip of whiskey.

Stone sat between his uncle and Matt, his gaze wavering between his clenched hands and Matt's face. 'How's your girl? Keeping out of trouble?'

Matt's jaw tightened. He didn't want to think about Jessie, or Stone, or Jethro. He needed to concentrate on his game, but just the mention of her tightened the knot of anxiety already sitting heavy in his belly.

Stone laughed and held out his hand. 'No hard feelings about what happened earlier, eh?' He touched the bandage taped to his ear. 'I see a pretty girl and . . . I guess I'm just used to getting what I want. Maybe I'll be luckier at cards.'

'I wouldn't count on it,' Langton said. 'Mr Lomew's won this game two years in a row. He's won big in Fletcher County, Carlton and Brinslow this year already.'

Stone nodded appreciatively. 'No wonder he's popular with the ladies.'

McCreedy tapped his fingers on the table, demanding attention. 'Well, you boys seem to know each other. Let me introduce you to everyone else.' He made the introductions then continued, 'And these two gentlemen are Mr Brown, of Brown's General Store and Haberdashery, and Mr Gold who owns the Beacon Hotel.'

The two men nodded and, after reaching under his seat, Brown handed a brown paper wrapped package across to Matt. 'I think this is yours. You dropped it outside my store earlier.'

The candy he had bought for Jessie. 'Thanks.'

McCreedy opened a new deck of cards, shuffled then handed it to Jethro for the cut. Everyone threw in the ante and the game got under way. Matt picked up a pair of queens off the deal. For the first few hands, he won a little, lost a little. One hour became three, each man suffering mixed fortunes, nobody gaining the upper hand. The man on the door brought food and whiskey, while McCreedy threw in anecdotes about his travels buying cattle. Nobody else said much.

Matt's pile of chips grew as he watched and listened. Brown played a careful game, winning and losing in equal amounts, but staying about even.

Gold had similar luck, although on a couple of occasions he seemed to fold too quickly when McCreedy raised. Langton seemed to enjoy watching the others. Judging by the diminished size of his pile of chips, his success with cards was limited to the luck of the draw.

And then there was Stone. He played like a child. His face lit up every time he had a hand and sank when he didn't. He bet on everything, and now, as they started the next round, he licked his lips as he looked hungrily at Matt's impressive winnings.

'You're sure living up to your reputation.' Stone glanced at the other players, seeking agreement and getting it. 'Seems like you have a lot of our money sitting on your side of the table.'

Matt hated chit-chat during a game at the best of times, and today wasn't one of those. He fought hard to keep his tone even. 'I don't chop wood for a living.'

Langton and McCreedy chuckled, both keeping their attention on their chips. Gold and Brown showed no signs of even hearing the conversation, although Matt doubted they missed anything.

Jethro whistled through his teeth. 'Good answer.'

'Are you too good for a hard day's work?' Stone asked. 'Or does it take more than a couple of dollars a day to keep that girl of yours happy? Ever thought she might like a man who gets his hands dirty?'

Matt's temper sizzled the way Stone probably intended, but he kept it under control. It was common enough for a man to try and distract an opponent, throw him off his game, but only a fool played into it. Besides, there was more than one way to shut Stone Davies up.

'Whose deal is it?' Matt asked.

'You gents ever met her?' Stone asked, downing another whiskey as he looked around the table at faces pinched with tension. 'You wouldn't forget her if you had. She looks like honey over warm apple pie. Smells good too, like flowers.'

'Sounds like a real lady. Lomew's obviously a lucky man,' Brown commented drily. 'Now are we here to talk or play cards?'

Stone ignored the hint. 'I bet underneath all that satin and lace she feels good too.'

Cards spilled across the table as Matt dropped the deck, coming stiffly to his feet, his right hand resting on his gun belt. 'Davies, I've listened to your talk for just about as long as I want to. If you've got something special you want to say to me or about me, that's fine. One thing you don't talk about is . . .' He stumbled over the name on the tip of his tongue, loath to give a face to Stone's filthy insinuations. 'You don't talk about a lady that way.'

Stone grinned, the effects of a full bottle of whiskey showing in his rosy cheeks. 'A lady? Well, ex-c-use me, I didn't know that. What's a body supposed to think when a girl stands outside a saloon like that?'

'Shut your filthy mouth!'

Stone held up his hands and looked around innocently at blank faces, finally meeting McCreedy's amused expression. 'I'm just saying—'

'Maybe you need to cool down, son,' McCreedy said, addressing his remark to Matt. 'We all heard what happened today and it stands to reason you'd be sore. No man likes to lose a fight, especially not in front of his girl. I never saw another man's business as being any of mine, never wanted to, but you kill a man at my table . . . that would surely spoil my game and then it would be my business.'

Langton nodded his agreement. Brown and Gold bowed their heads lower. Stone seemed suddenly interested in his filthy fingernails. Beside McCreedy, Jethro relaxed in his chair, his face a mask of indifference except for a challenging twinkle in his eyes.

Matt cursed his own stupidity. He should have guessed they would be playing him from the beginning. Glancing at Stone, he noticed he didn't look half as drunk now. *Idiot!* How the hell had he underestimated them that badly? Far from being the nonsensical ramblings of a drunk, Stone's constant stream of insinuations had undoubtedly been leading to this. Whatever Matt decided to do next, he would lose face, maybe even his liberty if he killed Stone the way he wanted to.

Going with his instincts, he sat down and swallowed some whiskey to ease his throat. 'I'm sorry, Mr McCreedy. I sure wouldn't want to spoil your game. Maybe I can make it up to you by giving you a chance to win back some of your money.'

Gold and Brown exchanged glances. Stone eyed his uncle sideways. But Jethro's gaze didn't falter as he nodded very slightly, almost approvingly.

'Apology accepted. It's your deal, Mr Lomew,' McCreedy reminded him.

Matt's enthusiasm for poker escaped him, but as he picked up the deck, shuffled and split it, another game occurred to him. Thumbing the first card, he deliberately hesitated. All attention fixed on him.

'Something wrong?' Jethro asked.

'What is it?' McCreedy asked.

'I don't know. It's just . . .' Matt considered his next words carefully, placing his gaze firmly with McCreedy. 'Well, the deck feels a little light.'

Clearing a space, Matt counted out the cards. 'Forty-nine, fifty . . .' He threw down the last card. 'Fifty-one.'

'How the hell could you have known that?' Stone asked, looking around the table as if for an answer. 'Nobody could . . . unless. . . .'

'Careful, son,' McCreedy warned. 'This is supposed to be a friendly game.'

'Friendly my ass. He's got most of our money sitting in front of him and suddenly the deck comes up short. I say—'

Jethro backhanded him across the chest, rocking him onto the back legs of his chair. 'Easy. Why would he say anything at all if he'd palmed a card?' He shook his head, apparently disgusted by his nephew's lack of reasoning. 'Who else in this room would have even noticed the deck was light?'

Mumbled agreements and synchronized head shaking confirmed it.

'Maybe it just fell out,' Matt said, pushing his chair back, 'when I dropped the deck.'

The other players moved back from the table, each man looking around the floor. Jethro leaned down towards his nephew's feet. It was a few seconds before he tossed the ace of hearts onto the table.

'Where'd you find it?' McCreedy asked.

Jethro narrowed his eyes at his nephew.

'Why the hell are you looking at me?' Stone lurched to his feet, his hand fanning towards his gun as his chair crashed over backwards. 'Are you trying to say I was cheating?'

'Easy, boys.' Without standing, McCreedy leaned across and rested his hand on Stone's gun arm. 'Like Mr Lomew said, it could have fallen out when he dropped the deck. No point getting excited about it.'

'I didn't notice, if it did,' Brown said, quietly.

'Me neither.' Langton eyed Stone's hand and continued to ease his chair away from the table. 'But it could have even fallen out of the shuffle.'

Matt raised an eyebrow.

'No offence, Mr Lomew,' Langton added.

'Or someone tossed it there when the deck turned up light,' Gold mumbled, looking directly at Stone.

'I ain't a cheat. Do you think I can't afford to lose a few dollars? Tell 'em, Jethro.' He glared at his uncle then looked for confirmation from every man in turn before settling his wrath on Matt. 'Maybe he put it there. You all saw the way he was looking for trouble with me.'

Gold looked up from his hands laid flat on the

table. 'Seems to me you're the one who's been doing all the riding tonight.'

'Me? All I done was talk about a pretty girl. When the hell was that ever a crime?' The fight dwindled from his voice to finish in a drunken whine.

Matt's hand rested on his thigh, close enough to draw his gun if he needed to. It itched to pummel Stone's face to a pulp, but until uncle or nephew made their move, he couldn't afford out-and-out trouble. For now, sleight-of-hand and Stone's humiliation at being branded a cheat would have to soothe his rancour.

He forced a smile. 'I'm here to play cards. That's all. I'm happy to accept it was an honest mistake if everyone else is.'

Stone stepped in closer, shaking with anger as he towered over Matt. 'Sounds like you're accusing me of something else. Is that right?'

Matt didn't move, just matched Stone's stare with insolent calm. 'Like I said, probably an honest mistake. Could happen to anyone. Why don't we just open a new deck and play on.'

Stone continued to glare, but the oppressive silence seemed to bother him. He looked around then turned to Jethro. 'I ain't no cheat and I ain't playing with cheats. Are you coming, Jethro?'

Jethro considered for a second or two then scooped his chips into his hat. 'I think maybe I will call it a night. Seems to me Matt's on a winning streak, and I believe I've seen enough for one evening.' He stood up, looking directly at Matt, the humour gone from his eyes despite the smile on his lips. 'It's been interesting. An education, you might say. I never before saw a man that quick with his hands. It's interesting to know.'

CHAPTER 7

After cashing in his chips, Jethro stopped at the crowded bar but, broke and humiliated, Stone was in no mood for idle chatter and a path cleared as he swept like a hurricane through the saloon. Not a man or woman seemed eager to voice an objection as he shoved them aside. Their fear warmed Stone, refuelling his confidence and stoking his vengeful streak.

'He's a slick son-of-a-bitch, I'll give him that,' he mumbled, as he stood in the street and spun the barrel of his six-shooter. 'I should have finished him when I had the chance. He's asking for it.'

He frowned as a few spots of rain wet his face, then crossed the street to the shelter of an abandoned doorway before he pulled a bag of makings from his coat and made a cigarette. Testily, he tried several times to strike a light before being successful, then for a few minutes stood in the shadows contemplating the day's events.

'Do you know what I think?' he asked aloud, flicking away his unlit smoke. 'I think he needs a better reason for me to kill him.'

He glanced around to make sure no one had overheard then smiled as he admired his logic. Jethro always said that most times a dead snake made more sense than he did but tonight he would show that mean old bastard. Show them all.

He lost his train of thought as he glimpsed a little redhead come out of the saloon, all breast and leg, definitely worth a second look. Any other time, she would be worth the couple of dollars it would cost him for the night, but tonight he had bigger plans and he forgot her once she disappeared into the shadows.

'One's pretty much like another when they're on their knees,' he muttered, scratching his crotch thoughtfully. 'Even Lomew's little bitch'll beg for it in the end.'

'That's a bad habit you've got there, Stone. I told you before: you need two people for a conversation.'

Stone turned on a dime, his hand sweeping down, ready to draw his gun. 'Is that you, Unc?'

Jethro stepped half into the light coming from a nearby lantern. 'I told you not to call me that.'

Stone relaxed. 'Who's going to hear?'

'I heard you making plans for Jessie Manners, didn't I?'

'Maybe,' Stone admitted with whiny reluctance. 'Or maybe I was just talking.'

He hated the way the old man made him feel three feet tall and five years old. Mean old bastard. He still hadn't told him why they hadn't killed

Lomew the minute they saw him. When Stone had asked, Jethro had told him to be patient. Well, that was all well and good when you had money in your pockets, but that game had about cleaned them out.

Jethro punched him on the arm. 'I hope so for your sake.'

Stone recognized the understated threat but curiosity outweighed good sense. 'Why? What's that supposed to mean?'

'Let's just say I don't want to see anything happen to that girl.'

Stone's jaw dropped. 'Any special reason why?'

'My interest is my business,' Jethro said evenly. 'And I'd advise you to start remembering that. Besides, you've got enough trouble with Matt Lomew without getting on the wrong side of me.'

Stone's hackles rose immediately. 'You're damned right. Son-of-a-bitch, making me look bad – twice. He's going to pay, big time.'

Jethro stepped back into the shadows. 'Are you going to shoot him in the back again?'

'You got that right. And this time I ain't so drunk I won't do the job right. This time I'm going to watch him die.'

Jethro sighed. 'Well, that's your business. Just leave the girl alone. Do you understand me?'

'Whatever you say, Unc, but can I at least have her when you're through with her?'

He didn't see it coming. He just felt the choking pressure of a forearm slammed across his throat. Heard the crack of wood as his back crashed painfully against a barred door. Every instinct told him to draw iron, kick, punch, gouge, or put up a fight of some kind but experience coupled with the weakness in his knees and the tingling sensation in his bladder were a compelling deterrent and he remained impassive.

'I don't think you're hearing me,' Jethro said, so close his breath felt moist against Stone's face. 'I said you don't touch her. Ever. Is that clear enough?'

Stone did his best to nod and the pressure eased, his knees buckling as they took his weight again. 'One of these days, Jethro,' he growled as he rubbed some feeling back into his bruised throat. He didn't have the nerve to finish his threat.

'I hear you,' he said. 'Hell, I never saw you take a real interest in a woman before. What kind of a nephew would I be to stand in the way now?'

He waited for an answer.

'Jethro? Are you there?'

Silence answered him and he breathed easier. Be patient, he warned himself. Someday soon Jethro would get what was coming to him, and even if it wasn't Stone who delivered the fatal blow, the satisfaction of seeing him dead would be the same.

Staring across at the saloon, he noticed the redhead leaning against the wall, smoking a cigarette, and smiled as he straightened his hat. The itch in his pants made him jig as he thought about the night he could have with her. Reaching into his pocket, he pulled out fluff and cursed. Lomew had cleaned him out to his last cent.

He watched the redhead toss her cigarette into the street and go back inside the saloon. *Shit.* He couldn't even afford a two-dollar whore.

'Damn you, Lomew. And damn you too, Jethro.'

He started down the street towards The Grand. What the hell right did Jethro have telling him what to do anyhow?

Leaving her bed, Jessie pulled a blanket with her and wrapped it around her shoulders. She had been tossing and turning for the past five hours if the clock on the dresser was to be believed. And she did. After the first two hours, she had left the lamp turned up so that she could count the minutes. Now with her mouth like cotton wool and her eyes sore from staring sightlessly at the ceiling, the time had come to give up hope of escaping into a dreamless sleep.

The same thoughts were still buzzing through her mind when she entered the kitchen, but she immediately forgot them when the door snapped shut behind her. Spinning around, the last person she expected to see was Stone Davies, but there he stood. With his back pressed against the wall, his arm across the door, he smiled wryly as he drew on a cigarette, watching her through the smoke tendrils as he exhaled.

'What are you doing here?' she asked, strangely annoyed rather than afraid to see him.

He pushed away from the wall and strolled to join her, backing her up to the table until she had nowhere to go unless she climbed over it. She raised her chin contemptuously, despite the overpowering size and nearness of him. Even when he pulled out a chair, turned it around, folded his arms across the back and straddled it, she didn't try to run. Later, she would probably wonder why she hadn't, but now, defiance held her in place. Or maybe it was curiosity and a misplaced belief in the good of mankind.

'Why are you here?'

'I came to see you. I thought we might get to know each other a little better.'

On another man, his grin might have been boyish, but on him it was evil. The way his gaze moved around her face, dipping to the open neck of her nightdress, she doubted his intentions were innocent. His lips glistened as his tongue flicked across them. Even his bobbing Adam's apple seemed to agree with her.

She clutched the neck of her gown together. 'It's late for a social call.'

'Less chance of us being disturbed.' He stared into her eyes, the mischief unmistakable in his. 'Don't even think about screaming.'

His fingers pushed hers aside, stroking her throat before curling around her neck and pulling her face closer to his. As his breath dampened her skin, panic finally kicked in and she strained against his hold.

'Don't do that, if you know what's good for you. I could snap your neck like a twig, but where would be the fun in that? It'd be better for both us if you just gave me some of that honey sweetness you're giving Lomew.'

The sour smell of liquor wafted into her nostrils bringing to mind an image formed years earlier of Ethan Davies, drunk and violent. With Stone's fingers sinking into her windpipe, choking off her air, she could almost believe it was the same man. Finally, her resolve not to provoke him, snapped. Indignation surged through her as she slapped at his hand, but he just held her wrist in a painful grip, twisting her arm until the pain crippled her into submission.

Somehow finding the strength to move beyond it, she lashed out. Her nails raked his cheek, blood beading instantly against his tanned skin. Calmly, he touched the cuts, scowling as he looked at the crimson coating his fingertips.

'That's not very friendly, but if that's the way you want to play it.'

She tried to yank away, but, as his chair overturned, he shoved her onto the table and pinned her arms. Bent over backwards, with her toes barely touching the freezing floor, his weight pressing down on her felt as though it would break her in half. With his cold lips suffocating her protests, her kicking and writhing only seemed to intensify the cruelty of his kiss.

'Jessie, is that you?'

Stone stepped away from her, one hand pressed against her chest, the other pressed to her lips while he tilted his good ear in the direction of the voice.

Beyond the kitchen, footsteps approached. Jessie recognized Lou's uneven lope and gave in to panic.

'Lou!'

Somehow she managed to duck free of Stone's restraint and tried to reach the hallway, but it was too late. As Stone's body slammed her against the wall, his bullets splintered the door. It creaked open giving Jessie a brief moment of hope before Lou staggered in, reeled against the table then crashed to the floor. Her stomach bucked, setting off a reaction that seemed to strip six years from her in a split second, leaving her physically sick as she watched a familiar scene played out with unfamiliar characters.

Stone's .45 dug into her cheek as he forced her to look. 'Hurts, doesn't it, to lose someone you care about?'

She screwed her eyes shut. *Wake up*. The familiar nightmare had to end now, didn't it? And yet this time it was different. The chaos around her continued. Stone shouted into her face but he might as well have been talking Apache. Nothing made sense. Only the blood seemed real.

'Look!' he screamed against her ear. 'Look! I want you to remember everything.'

She fought him, spinning until her face was only inches away from his. 'I do remember everything, you son-of-a bitch.' Her spittle flecked his cheek. 'Do you think this is the first time I've seen a man gunned down in cold blood? You're just like your father. A murderer. And just like Ethan Davies you'll get what's coming to you when Matt finds you.'

'Lomew?' He seemed genuinely amused. 'He's a dead man walking.'

She laughed in his face. 'You're no match for Matt. He'll kill you exactly the way he killed your pa. And I'll watch and—'

He punched her so hard she crumpled. As he picked her up and carried her away, the last thing she saw was Lou, face down on the floor in a pool of blood. As he carried her out into the wind and rain, darkness finally eased the pain and she slipped gratefully into unconsciousness.

CHAPTER 8

Carrying the candy, Matt stepped out of the oppressive atmosphere of the gaming room and sucked in the crisp night – early morning – air. Somewhere along the street, a volley of gunshots disturbed the otherwise perfect silence and he shook his head thoughtfully. Some towns never seemed to sleep, but then in his line of work that wasn't a bad thing. Maybe he should settle down here if he lived through all this. No, not maybe. Definitely. With a receipt from Langton in his pocket for almost $25,000 and a gutful of whiskey blurring the line between possible future outcomes, the only thing left to do before he turned in for eight hours of well-deserved sleep was give Jess her birthday present.

Feeling younger than he had in a long time, he tripped off the plank walk ankle-deep into a pile of manure. Like a drunken fool, he chuckled as he shook his boot. Was that meant to be good luck? Whether it was or not, his day hadn't turned out too badly and if he could make things right with Jess, then he could face whatever tomorrow – today –

threw at him. He started to walk, taking two decisive strides before a voice stopped him.

'Matt, you forgot this.'

He turned slowly, only just recognizing Jethro through the encroaching darkness. The dim light coming from the saloon's grimy windows revealed him standing on the edge of the shadows, forever watchful as he surveyed the street along its length and breadth and back again. He held out Matt's cane.

Matt stared at the damn thing for a few seconds, saying nothing when he finally took it.

'You're welcome. How's the girl?' Jethro asked, as if he was an old family friend.

If Jethro's unexpected appearance hadn't sobered him up, that question did. For a moment Matt was at a disadvantage as he wondered where Stone was. Moving in behind him, already aiming a bullet at the centre of his back?

'Take it easy, Matt. Stone's off whoring somewhere and when the time comes, you and I will meet in a fair fight. Right now, all I'm doing is returning something that belongs to you.'

The assurance didn't do much for Matt's confidence and he kept his thumb resting lightly on his belt buckle as he stared back at Jethro, the awkward silence spoiling his mood.

'Well then, if you'll excuse me. . . .' he said, eventually.

Jethro stepped forward, his arms folded across his chest, a sudden sense of urgency about him, as if he had just reached a decision. 'How much do you know about that girl of yours? Where she came from? Who she is?'

Enough that he didn't want to share. 'That's my business, not something I want to discuss with a man who's made it clear he wants to take my girl and my life and probably not in that order.'

Jethro nodded agreeably, backing off slightly as he relaxed visibly. 'That's fair enough. How about this then: have you asked yourself why I haven't killed you yet?'

Matt managed to keep his pride in check. After all, in a fair fight he wasn't sure he could beat Jethro to the draw. 'Haven't given it a thought. You'll call it when you're ready, I guess.'

Jethro frowned. 'You're a cool customer. Usually, I like that in a man, but on you it's a little ... unnerving.'

The admission surprised Matt. He hadn't thought for a minute that Jethro might be experiencing the same feelings of doubt that he himself was.

'You see, emotions weaken a man,' Jethro said. 'Especially love. Do you know what I'm saying? Are you a weak man, Matt?'

The questions were undoubtedly meant to make Matt uncomfortable and his palm felt sticky against the candy melting inside its wrapper. 'Can't say as I've noticed,' he said with as much nonchalance as he could muster.

'There you go again, making me want to like you.' Jethro unfolded his arms and let his hands hang loose at his sides. 'Watch your back, Matt Lomew,' he said, as he walked away.

Matt pulled up his collar against a sudden chill and the patter of rain, and contemplated Jethro. Matt had no idea what the hell that little pow-wow was all about, but he decided that at least for tonight Jethro posed no threat to him or Jessie. Strange that he should take the word of an outlaw but Jethro was a notorious bad man with a reputation built on instilling fear. When he eventually decided to make his play, it would be in full view of witnesses who could keep that legend alive. Maybe tomorrow Matt would feel differently, but tonight while his brain was addled with expensive booze he had things to straighten out with Jessie.

In the few minutes it took to walk to the hotel, Matt couldn't come up with one reasonable excuse he could give to Lou as to why he needed to see Jessie in the middle of the night. And he had no doubt Lou would be waiting for him. After all, he had put up the $5000 dollars that got Matt into the game, and being a shrewd businessman he'd want to know what the return was on his investment. Treading softly, Matt approached the abandoned desk, smiling at the open book of Shakespeare and half-empty cup of coffee. Yep. Lou was nothing if not predictable.

Voices coming from the dining room, or maybe the kitchen, made him hesitate. He hadn't expected anybody but Lou to be up this late, but it sounded like quite a party and, as he glanced towards the stairs, he saw the shadows of more people coming down. Quickly, he headed along a narrow corridor to the rear of the reception, passing several doors before he reached a room at the end. Light seeped out to meet him, and without hesitation, he tapped and pressed himself close against the panels as he glanced back towards the busy lobby.

'Jess,' he whispered into the wood. 'It's Matt. Let me in.'

Inside, nothing stirred. He knocked again, waiting a couple of seconds before finding the handle and trying it. The door opened and he peered inside. The room was empty, although the bed was mussed. Shoving back the blankets, he pressed his palm to the sheet. Cold. So, Lou wasn't the only one waiting up for him and he bet he knew exactly where to find them both. Jess loved a party.

Leaving the room as he found it, he closed the door and headed towards the noise. The first person he met was the sheriff. Although only in his late thirties, the sheriff's face wore the ravages of a man much older and rarely showed any signs of humour. Tonight he looked more dour than usual.

'I didn't expect to find you here at this time, Sheriff. What's the occasion?'

Matt looked past him towards the crowd converging on them and something cold settled inside him. Since when did people go to a party wearing nightdresses and bed shirts? And a gloomier looking bunch he couldn't remember seeing.

The sheriff placed a huge hand on his arm. 'It's Lou.'

Matt scanned the faces bearing down on him, seeing none he recognized. 'Where is he? What's happened?'

'Kitchen. I'm sorry, Lomew. He's dead.'

Matt exploded through the crowd, shaking off hands that tried to hold him back. He smelled the blood before he reached the kitchen and his stomach tightened in a hard knot. It wasn't the first time he had seen a dead man – he had sent a few on their way – but Lou was his friend and seeing his corpse amidst the carnage pulled him up short and sober.

He gripped the door, or what was left of it, swaying as it moved under his weight. Inside, he burned with a rage that made him want to destroy everything and everyone around him. On the outside, utter stillness enveloped him. With a glance, he noticed a spray of blood on the wall, muddy boot prints entering and leaving by the back door and smaller bare footed prints mixed in.

The sheriff squeezed past him, reaching under the table to retrieve a blanket which he draped over Lou's corpse. As the bright colours swam before Matt's eyes, a spark of recognition pulsed through him. Dropping to his knees, he grasped the corner of the blanket, thrusting it towards the sheriff like an accusation.

'Where's Jessie?'

'Wasn't she with you?'

'No.' Suspicion crossed his mind. 'Stone Davies. Has anybody seen him?'

A few murmurs offered no help.

'If we find him, we'll find her and Lou's killer,' Matt opined, without hesitation or doubt.

'What makes you so sure?' the sheriff asked.

Matt checked his gun. In his mind the stupidity of the question defied an answer. Or maybe the sheriff was in on it. *No.* That was his frustration talking. He needed to calm down, think straight.

'I said, what makes you so sure?'

Matt concentrated on his weapon, struggling to contain his agitation as his hand shook. 'You heard about the run in I had with him today?'

The sheriff nodded.

'Then you know he wanted her. Tonight, at Hank McCreedy's game, he was riding me with filthy hints and accusations about her.'

'A few words don't make a man guilty of kidnapping and murder.'

Matt pointed to the confusion of prints on the wooden floor. 'Maybe this'll help to convince you. One set of boots come in, one set goes out.' He gestured to the smaller prints. 'Here, bare feet. I don't see them leave. To me, that means she's still here, or she was carried out. Do you see her?'

The sheriff scowled. 'What makes you think they're her prints?'

A sigh punctuated Matt's impatience. Why the hell was he even bothering to try and explain to this imbecile when he couldn't see what was right before his face? Obviously the sheriff would sooner be sitting in his office with his feet on his desk and his hat pulled low than actually earning his forty dollars a month.

'Forget it.' Matt rammed his gun into its holster. 'I'll find her.'

'All I'm saying is—'

'He's right, Sheriff.'

Matt didn't need to turn around to recognize Jethro's drawl or to know that a space had cleared around them.

'Stone came for the girl and he took her. This man probably just got in the way.'

The sheriff's mistrust was evident as he peered past Matt's shoulder and frowned. 'I thought Stone Davies was your nephew. It seems strange you'd be helping Lomew lay the blame on him.'

Jethro shrugged non-committally.

'All right, assuming you're on the level, what makes you so sure?'

Dropping to his haunches, Jethro drew a circle in the muddy tracks. 'See this?'

Matt and the sheriff leaned in closer, both nodding at the thin line Jethro pointed to in a bare heel print.

'Glass. When the girl was three years old, she stepped on a broken bottle. That's the scar. Now, like Lomew said, you find Stone and you'll find her . . . and knowing my nephew like I do, you don't have a lot of time.'

A few people in the group crowding in behind them started whispering and a woman started to cry. Seeming to thaw a little, the sheriff continued to stare thoughtfully at the evidence. Beneath his calm exterior, Matt's curiosity escalated. How could Jethro know about a scar on Jessie's foot, and if what he said was true, how did he know how it got there? He left the questions unasked, willing to buy into Jethro's story if it meant the sheriff would act.

'Now do you believe me?' he asked.

'I never doubted you, Mr Lomew, but I'm the law and I have to follow the evidence.' He switched his attention to Jethro. 'You seem to know quite a bit about what might have happened here, makes me wonder if you didn't have some part in it.'

A slight twitch around the eyes was the only sign that Jethro resented the accusation. 'I was with Lomew when it happened. We were outside the Big Nugget when we heard the shots.'

'Convenient the way you kept me talking,' Matt said, thoughtfully. 'Makes me wonder if the sheriff might not be right about you and Stone planning this all along. Maybe taking Jessie is just part of your plan to kill me.'

'I thought you had more brains than that, but if that's how you feel. . . .'

Jethro turned to walk away but Matt jabbed him in the stomach with his cane, driving him back against the wall before bringing the stick up across Jethro's chest and pinning him with the full weight of his body. 'Where is she, Jethro? Where's he taken her?'

Jethro's eyes twinkled. 'You want to let me go before you do something you regret.'

'If he hurts her . . .' Matt leaned in closer. 'I'll—'

Matt felt his legs kicked from under him and then he was on his back, Jethro's knee wedged across his throat and his own .45 pressed against his cheek.

'You're weak, Matt. You can't protect her if you're weak.'

A gun muzzle appeared at Jethro's temple. 'Let him up, Davies,' the sheriff said, cocking his six-shooter.

Jethro grinned and stood up as if his actions had been nothing more than a friendly tussle. For a moment he hung onto Matt's Colt, weighing it in his hand before hanging it from his finger and handing it back to him. After Matt took it and slipped it in its holster, Jethro held out his hand.

'You need my help if you want to see the girl alive again, so swallow your pride and take my hand. I won't offer it a second time.'

Matt looked long and hard into the face of the man who only hours earlier had promised to kill him, had publicly beaten him and whose reputation alone as a cold-blooded killer could instil fear in the most vicious outlaw. A man who had seemed to revel in pouring scorn on a nephew no less dangerous and certainly more volatile than himself.

With a bad feeling gnawing at the pit of his stomach, he grasped Jethro's arm and hauled himself up. 'Don't think this means I trust you.'

'Good. You shouldn't.'

Matt's jaw crackled as he ground his teeth against a swell of doubt. 'We're wasting time. Sheriff?'

The lawman hesitated, but with the crowd moving

restlessly and two men arming up for a fight, possibly with each other, he seemed disinclined to argue any further.

'Well, you boys seem to have a plan, unlikely as that seems to me.' He pushed past them, towards the hallway and into the restless crowd. 'Anyone who wants to join the search, make yourself decent and meet me in front of the hotel in five minutes.'

Matt started to follow but changed his mind and instead headed for the back door. Jethro followed on his heels like a noon shadow. As Matt yanked open the door, they braced against a torrent of rain that swept in on a fierce gust of wind.

'Hell of a night for playing find the needle in the haystack,' Jethro commented.

Matt turned up his collar and faced into the darkness. 'If you want to change your mind, that's up to you. Just don't get in my way.'

CHAPTER 9

Half an hour later, Matt met up with Jethro in the middle of Main Street.

'Did you find anything?' Matt asked.

'Nothing. The woman who runs the boarding-house where we've been staying said she hasn't seen him, and reminded me we owed her four nights' rent. The sheriff's still there, keeping an eye on the place. You?'

Matt shook his head. 'I went to the livery stable and nobody's ridden in or out of town since last night so far as I can tell. I ran into the owner of the general store and some of the others on the way here, they've been checking anywhere a man might hide and there's no trace. Nobody's seen hide nor hair of him or Jessie. It's like they just fell off the face of the earth.'

Matt didn't want to admit it, but the situation didn't look good. If Stone's own blood-kin couldn't find him, what chance did the rest of them have? Unless Jethro was playing them. Even if he was, the sheriff had sent men to watch all the routes out of town from north to south, east and west, although in truth a man could ride out almost unseen if he wanted to risk it. With dawn still an hour away, even if he did leave a trail it would be impossible to track him until then.

'I'll keep looking. If he's in town, I'll find him,' Jethro said. 'If he isn't, you can hunt him down until you do.'

Matt couldn't help but try to satisfy a question that had been burning through his mind like a brand. 'I thought you Davieses were meant to be close as ticks on a dog?'

Jethro nodded, his attention focused more on the street than Matt.

'Then why are you helping me track down Stone?'

'Let's just say there's blood and then there's blood.'

It didn't make any sense, and with the whiskey wearing off, Matt's patience was wearing thin. He turned away, too quickly, only Jethro's hand gripping him by the elbow keeping him upright as he struggled to keep his balance in the sucking mud. Angrily, he snatched free. 'I don't need your help.'

Jethro's eyes narrowed as he looked him up and down and he seemed to hesitate. 'I didn't have anything to do with that trouble you had in Silver Springs. I hear Stone put three bullets in you.'

'Four,' Matt said, drily.

'Sounds like Stone. He's like his pa. No finesse. Still, when a man lives through a thing like that, it must take a lot out of him. Maybe you should take the weight off for a minute or two. You won't be any good to the girl if—'

'Don't waste your concern on me, I'm fine.' It was a lie but pride wouldn't let Matt admit to the pain gnawing at his back and sapping the strength from his legs. He would like nothing more than to give in to it, but he couldn't. 'You just worry about finding Stone before I do.'

'Have it your own way, but it wouldn't do any harm to check she isn't back at the hotel.'

Matt's frustration with the easy way Jethro read him, simmered close to boiling, but he kept it below the surface. After all, for whatever reason, Jethro appeared to be trying to help him find Jessie. Matt couldn't help wondering about that, his silence rebuilding the tension between them as he half turned to leave. One thing was sure, whatever Jethro's plans were, they didn't include saying more than he needed to. And if he was on the level, they probably didn't include Jessie being taken by Stone either. If nothing else, Jethro was a straight shooter and Matt counted on that as he maintained a nerve-racking silence. Whatever thoughts were crossing Jethro's mind, nothing showed on his face as he matched Matt's stare with one of mild amusement before turning away and heading off into the night.

Back at the hotel, Matt could still picture that secretive little smile that said Jethro had at least one ace up his sleeve. Slamming the door shut behind him, he kept his focus on the street as he drank a long measure of laudanum. It was something he tried not to do, but his back felt close to breaking and his legs trembled with each step. Until he found Jessie, he couldn't afford the luxury of weakness. He remembered again what the doctor in Silver Springs had told him as he mounted the stage to leave.

'*You know you should still be taking it easy. It isn't just about the skin healing. Bullets tear up your insides and—*'

'*I know, Doc. Plenty of rest.*'

Matt corked the bottle and slipped it back deep inside his saddle-bag. He would consider the advice some other time. Right now, he needed to find Jessie. If anything happened to her, nothing else would matter anyway. The realization stopped him in his tracks. He had been right when he said she clouded his judgement, but hadn't she always?

He slipped his gun from its holster, checking the chambers. For a moment, he hesitated before sliding it home again, the same feelings of doubt he had experienced earlier creeping back into his thoughts. A reputation based on a quick draw and a few fancy tricks was all well and good, but he had sworn a long time ago never to take another man's life. Would he have the guts to do it now? Was he fast enough to take Jethro Davies down when the time came?

Turning away from the window, he reached into his saddle-bag and withdrew another Colt, older and scarred, but nonetheless clean and loaded. This one, he tucked into the back of his pants before a rapid tap at the door made him freeze.

'It's Jethro. You better come quick. The sheriff's got Stone pinned down at the boarding-house.'

Jethro staggered back as the door swung open.

'You said he wasn't there,' Matt said, unable to hide the accusation. 'Is Jessie with him?'

'We don't know.'

Matt grabbed his coat and hat off the bed, putting them on as they ran through the hotel and out into the street. The wind that had tickled his neck earlier, battered him now, like invisible hands trying to hold him back, but he forced against it and headed towards the sunrise. *Sunrise?* That couldn't be right, and there was a distinct smell of smoke on the air.

He arrived at the boarding-house a few steps behind Jethro, breathing hard. Men including the patrons of the saloon next door had formed a ragged bucket line but already flames engulfed the first floor of the lodgings. Dangerous red embers hissed into the night, forcing back anyone foolhardy enough to challenge them.

'Is he in there?' Matt gasped out, avoiding the real question as he leaned on the sheriff for support. He hated his cane, but he could do with it now as his body threatened to buckle.

The sheriff looked at him sideways. 'Nobody saw him come out. That feller Brown who owns the store managed to get in before the fire took hold.' The sheriff shook his head. 'I think I saw him come out. I've been too busy trying to put these flames out to notice much else.' He stepped back as a fiery splinter arced towards his feet. 'Jesus!'

Any other time, Matt might have laughed at the sheriff's self-important incompetence but a question hotter than the fire burned on the tip of his tongue. 'What about Jessie?'

The sheriff swallowed a few times, his eyes bulging as his attention fastened on the scene before them. While they stood and watched, windows exploded as the heat intensified, leaving smoke blackened and fire singed curtains to billow forlornly into the night. Within seconds the intensity of the heat had already caused the paint around the frames to blister and the sound of wood splintering punctuated the cries of the frantic townspeople.

The sheriff shouted a few instructions to the bucket line to wet down the buildings either side of the boarding-house. When nobody seemed to take any notice, he started forward, trying to resist Matt who held him back.

'Has anyone seen Jessie yet?'

'We're not sure,' he said with obvious reluctance. 'It-it could have been her. It could have been anyone.'

'Where?' Despite the searing heat, foreboding chilled Matt to the bone.

'At one of the upstairs windows, before the fire took hold.'

Now it was Matt's turn to break for the house. This time the sheriff grabbed him. 'It could have been Mrs Donovan, the owner. No one's seen her yet. Just let us—'

A crash turned their attention back to the flaming building. Someone was trying to kick through the door from the inside. After several attempts the scorched wood gave way and a flaming apparition barely recognizable as Brown staggered out carrying a woman over his shoulder.

By the time Matt lunged to the fore, Jethro had already tackled Brown to the ground and was rolling him and the woman in the mud. As the flames died, someone else threw wet blankets over the pair. As the stench of scorched flesh reached his nostrils, Matt pulled up short, paralysed with fear like nothing he had ever known.

Dropping onto one knee, Jethro raised his hands helplessly as Brown writhed and screamed in agony. A red-headed man Matt recognized as the town's doctor, knelt beside the woman. Unlike Brown, she lay still, her clothes in shreds, her body blistered and sooty, her hair all but burnt away leaving behind only the charred remains of her flesh. Matt reeled as the young MD covered her over fully with the blanket. A woman started crying. Hands clutched at him as the world tilted, but he shoved them away, fighting his way back from the brink of physical and mental collapse.

Somewhere on the edge of his comprehension, Matt heard a man say, 'I think it's Mrs Donovan.' He started to breathe again, deep then shallow as the ember-filled air attacked his lungs.

'Look! Up there,' someone shouted.

His gaze shifted to the second storey, scanning the windows where a rosy tinge added life to the drifting smoke that weaved its way ever upwards, guiding the hungry flames to new feeding grounds. At first, he saw nothing. And then, he spotted hands pressed against glass and the faintest shadow of a face.

He couldn't say where his strength came from. Maybe it was blind panic that drove him though the crowd, onto the steps of the saloon, onto the porch railing and up onto the overhang. The distance between the saloon and the boarding-house was just a few feet and without thinking of the consequences he threw himself across. The wood sagged under his weight, but held, and he didn't linger. The window where he had seen the woman was closest to him. Peering inside he saw nothing through the smoke.

He smashed the glass with his elbow, ducking quickly to the side as smoke and heat rushed out. Beneath his feet the overhang creaked and he dived in through the window, landing flat on his face. Staying low, he looked around at floor level where the smoke was thinnest, the air almost breathable. On the second sweep, he saw a figure hunched beside the window and crawled back towards it.

'Jessie?' he asked, already knowing it wasn't her. This woman was too broad. Fear-filled eyes glistened back at him. 'Mrs Donovan?' he asked, dreading the answer.

She nodded, reigniting the fear and suspicion that had paralysed him so completely when the doctor covered the corpse in the street.

'We're trapped,' Mrs Donovan, croaked. 'We're going to die.'

'No, we aren't. Now get up and climb through the window.'

'My leg is hurt. I can't stand on it.'

'Then wrap your arms around my neck because burning isn't the way I intend to die and I'm not leaving without you.'

Her teeth flashed against the sootiness of her skin, then reluctantly, she did as he bid, crying against his ear as he gathered her into her arms.

'Now close your eyes, take a breath and hold it for as long as you can. Ready?'

He felt her chest heave against his, and followed his own advice as he staggered to his feet. As they left the band of cleaner air, a cloud of black smoke cloaked them. Matt blinked rapidly. His eyes watered, blinding him as ash and smoke attacked them. He paused a moment to get his bearings. The window had been behind him. Had he turned as he lifted Mrs Donovan? He forced himself to stop and listen, being repaid by the sound of voices coming from . . . his left?

Mrs Donovan choked against his ear. Stumbling backwards a couple of paces, he reeled, touching the wall with his left shoulder. He stepped back again and again, suddenly losing his precarious balance as the wall disappeared.

Sensing the window, he slipped his backside onto the ledge, glass shards tearing his pants as he pulled his legs around awkwardly and negotiated himself and Mrs Donovan out. Looking down into the street, his eyes barely open, he glimpsed a crowd of men below shouting unintelligibly and waving up at him.

Tentatively, he tested his foot on the wooden

overhang. It creaked but held. Unsteadily, he lowered his weight onto it. Mrs Donovan's nails cut into his neck as he eased his way along the wall, keeping close as a coat of paint to the blistering wood frontage.

'The porch is about to go,' someone shouted.

Through slitted eyes, his gaze followed the direction of the voice and he glimpsed two men, standing on the porch of the saloon. How he had reached the gap between the buildings so quickly he had no idea, but as he teetered near the edge he felt the wood give way beneath his feet. He started to fall, felt Mrs Donovan lose her grip and heaved her towards the men. She screamed, but there was nothing he could do as the roof finally gave way and he plunged blindly into a heap of new pain and defeat.

CHAPTER 10

From an abandoned warehouse opposite the boarding house, Jessie watched as Matt climbed the roof, emerging from the burning building minutes later with a woman she recognized as the proprietor. When the roof collapsed, burying him under its smouldering wreckage, she screamed against the gag cutting into her mouth, and renewed her struggles against the ties binding her hands and feet.

It earned her another slap and her breathing quickened along with her heartbeat as she listened to Stone chuntering. Morning was rushing in on them now, giving detail to the grey-clad shadows and allowing her to see his hands shaking as he checked the chambers of his gun. Her mind scrambled for a plan, but beyond the cold gnawing at her and the throb in her jaw, nothing else registered clearly.

Nothing except the gun.

She tried again to scream but the attempt stuck in her throat, the pathetic choking sound drawing Stone's attention and with it the muzzle of the weapon. Suddenly, her bound limbs moved of their own accord, taking her awkwardly backwards as she scrambled for cover that didn't exist.

'Just you and me now,' Stone said, holstering the gun as he strode towards her.

She ducked sideways as he grabbed for her but with her hands and feet tied she had no chance of escaping. Until she saw a blade flash in his hand. Somehow, she managed to roll out of his reach but it was a short-lived bid for freedom as he tackled her onto her stomach, his knee digging painfully into the small of her back.

Suddenly, she felt the painful pressure at her ankles ease followed by an intense tingling in her wrists as her hands fell free. Immediately, she clawed at the dirt floor, trying to pull herself free of his weight.

Yanking hard on her hair, he snatched her back. 'Where do you think you're going?' He nicked her cheek with the blade as he sliced through the gag, allowing her to spit it out before his hand tightened around her throat.

'Ain't any use trying to call for help. There's so much going on out there, so many men shouting, women screaming, nobody's going to hear you above a hullabaloo like that.'

He was right. They were so close and yet they could have been a mile away. Nobody was coming to help her. Her fate was in her own hands.

'Please, let me go,' she gasped, her reasoning being her only bargaining chip. 'You can get away while they're busy trying to put out the fire.'

Stone laughed. 'Nice try.'

'I promise, I won't tell them anything.' She stopped struggling as the breath in her body dwindled.

'I don't need your promises.' He shifted his weight from her back and turned her over to face him. 'When I'm through with you. . . .'

The desires of men were a mystery to her, but Jessie knew instinctively what Stone intended. Maybe it was the wild, hungry look in his eyes, or the tautness of his body as he dragged her against him. Maybe it was just the worst thing she could imagine.

'You can't do this,' she said, fighting against him.

He stopped as if to consider the possibility, drawing the Bowie knife gently along the profile of her face before stabbing it into the dirt beside her head. 'Give me one good reason why the hell not?'

'Because . . . I'm your cousin, Jessica-Rose.' Even now, with her life depending on it, she almost choked on the words, still half-refusing to believe the suspicions that her conversation with Jethro had thrown up. But what did it matter what she believed as long as Stone did?

His laugh was one of genuine amusement. 'Wondered when you'd get round to admitting that.'

The realization that he already seemed to know momentarily replaced fear with curiosity.

'You knew?'

Stone smiled but it didn't reach his eyes. 'There ain't no other reason I've been tagging along with Jethro for so long. I knew sooner or later, he'd find you.'

'You've been looking for me?' It didn't make sense, especially with him about to defile and probably kill her. 'What did I ever do to you?'

'Nothing.'

'Then why—'

'Because Jethro did.' A faraway look came into his eyes. 'And payback's a bitch.'

She managed to wrap her fingers around the knife just before her head jarred against the ground and, as he came down on her, she lashed out. The knife raked across his forehead, his nose and down his cheek. Sticky warmth splashed her lips and she gagged on the metallic taste of his blood.

He gripped her wrist, easily taking the knife from her tenuous grasp. 'You little hellcat.'

The blade flashed close to her eye before spinning off to a point behind them. Glass shattered.

'Shit. Now look what you made me do.'

He slapped her across the jaw, again and again, leaving her dazed and unable to resist when his hand clamped her wrists above her head, exposing her fully to his insane pawing. His laughter mocked her, his physical anger quickly weakening her frenzied attempts to escape. It was useless. He was twice her size and driven insane by hatred she couldn't even begin to understand.

She stopped struggling and spat blood in his face. 'What did Jethro ever do to you?'

'He took what should have been mine.'

His mouth came down hard on hers as it twisted with disgust, his stubble rasping her face and renewing her struggles. She sank her teeth into his lip. He moved quickly, his forearm choking her as it slammed across her throat. Trapped, she couldn't breathe, couldn't fight anymore.

'That's better. Now you just lie still 'cause I ain't got time for games now. And don't think you ain't got nothing to lose by fighting me. You see, I ain't going to kill you. I need you alive for what I've got planned.'

He eased the pressure on her throat, allowing her to gasp in a few breaths of smoky air. 'Don't do this to me. It's not right. I'm your cousin. I never did anything to you.'

His laughter mocked her as he unbuttoned his pants. 'Maybe, maybe not, but you've been company with them that did. You see, Lomew might have fired the bullet that killed my pa but Jethro was the man who destroyed him.'

CHAPTER 11

For a few seconds, Matt didn't feel anything as he lay motionless beneath the smouldering remains of the porch. The fall seemed to have knocked every ache and emotion from him and, as he opened his eyes, he wondered if he were still alive, or if the lightening sky was the doors of Heaven opening to let him in.

And then all hell broke loose.

He gasped, unable to draw breath, aware only of a crushing weight across his chest. Frantically, he clawed at the scorching wood, his fingers stinging then burning. His whole body felt as if it was on fire, the stench of searing flesh filling his nostrils as he fought helplessly to free himself. Suddenly the weight lifted and for a split second he believed he was floating. Then hard earth slammed against his back and a new screeching, winged enemy battered him.

'That's enough. Do you want to kill him?' Someone knelt at his side and spoke close to his ear. 'Matt, can you hear me?'

His eyelids fluttered, refusing to open fully as a

familiar face swam in and out of focus and Jethro peered intently down at him. Immediately, Matt tried to get up but a stabbing pain in his back, and Jethro's hand pressed firmly against his shoulder, stopped him.

'Don't try to move,' Jethro warned. 'The doctor's coming.'

Ignoring his advice, Matt grabbed the front of Jethro's coat. 'We need to find Jessie.'

Jethro gripped his arm, shaking his head as he knelt beside him and pushed him down. 'You need to take it easy, son. That was a hell of a fiery fall you just took.'

Matt struggled to focus then closed his eyes against the annoying blur of colour that made his stomach undulate. In a world of darkness he noticed his own rapid breathing and tried in vain to lengthen the quick breaths that tugged him close to unconsciousness. The sound of breaking glass mingled with a scream echoing through the blackness, jolted him back to full awareness with the surety of a bucket of cold water thrown in his face. Stubbornly, he forced his eyelids to open and stay open.

'What is it? What did you see?' he asked, noticing Jethro's gaze stray to a point behind him.

'Nothing.'

Matt secured his grip on Jethro before he could get away. 'You heard Jessie scream, didn't you?'

Jethro hesitated. 'No. Women are having hysterics all over the place.'

'You're lying. What did you see?' He tensed as pain streaked through him, spreading from the tips of his blistered fingers out to every inch of his body as he struggled to stop Jethro leaving. His fingertips burned white hot as he fumbled with the thong on his holster but the Colt slipped easily into his hand. 'You know where they are, don't you? Help me, God damn you,' he said, pressing the muzzle to Jethro's side, 'or I'll shoot you dead and crawl over your corpse if I have to.'

'Don't be a fool. You're in no condition to go anywhere. Let the doctor tend to you and I'll bring Jess back.'

'What about Stone? Will you bring him back?'

Jethro's mouth puckered into a scowl, his answer clear in the twitch at the corner of his eye.

'That's what I thought. Now, help me up.' He pushed the muzzle of the Colt tighter against Jethro's side. 'I won't ask again.'

'All right.' Jethro waited for the .45 to drop. 'But next time you pull that iron, make sure you use it. You might not get a second chance.'

Matt didn't actually see the short punch that connected with his jaw, but he felt its power just before he slipped into oblivion.

'Stone? Are you in there?'

Jessie waited for the next blow to fall, but Stone's raised fist stopped in mid-air. Looking past his elbow, she barely made out Jethro moving in behind him and her hopelessness hit rock bottom.

100

'What the hell did you do to her?' Jethro asked, running the last few feet to crouch beside her.

Although Stone had failed in his attempts to exact his punishment completely, that had only increased his cruelty as he beat her nearly senseless. Through eyes swollen almost shut, she thought she saw concern on Jethro's face as he squinted down at her. But it didn't stop her cringing when he pushed Stone aside and gathered the remnants of her nightdress around her.

'You mean son-of-a-bitch,' he said. 'She didn't deserve this.'

'The hell she didn't.' Stone wiped his eye as he thrust his chin forward to display the ugly slash dripping blood down his face. 'Look what she did to me.'

Uncoiling like a spring, Jethro landed a fist to Stone's chin that sent him flying backwards and crashing into a rotten wooden crate. For a brief moment, it looked like Stone wouldn't get up as he shook splinters out of his hair and gingerly massaged his jaw.

'What was that for?' he asked, reeling to his feet.

'I told you not to touch her.'

'Yeah, you did, didn't you?' He hitched his pants up higher at the waist and scratched his crotch. 'I guess I forgot.'

Jethro glanced at Jessie, and for a split second she recalled seeing that same look of sadness before. The day her mother had died. He had looked at her that way and even at the age of four she had known that

101

nothing was ever going to be the same again. And it wouldn't be now. She dropped her gaze, wishing for some release from the hopeless situation she was in, but the throbbing in her head refused to let her go.

'Stone, you better get out of here,' Jethro opined. 'It won't be long 'til Lomew comes round and tells them where to find you.'

Jessie teetered back from her hazy reality, meeting Stone's ugly glare with what she hoped was one of triumph.

'He's still alive? Good. I was worried that fall might have killed him, robbed me of seeing him die for what he did to me and my pa.'

'Forget him,' Jethro said, off-handedly. 'He's crippled. That fall finished the work your bullets started.'

'If he ain't dead, that means he's alive. Alive's still breathing and I swore on my pa's grave the man who killed him wouldn't draw another breath when I found him.'

Jethro's sigh was audible, even over the chaos outside surrounding the fire.

'You know, Unc, I don't think you feel as strongly about it as I do. In fact, you've been riding drag ever since you saw this girl. Maybe you've got some business you need to take care of.' He broke into a lascivious grin and half-turned towards the door. 'I can keep watch if you want to scratch an itch with the brat.'

Even Jessie knew it was a trap.

'Shut your filthy mouth or. . . .' Jethro's gun hand

twitched but he let the threat hang and instead straightened his hat as he stood up.

'Or what?' Stone asked, squaring up, back straight, legs slightly bent, hand shifting lazily to shadow his gun. 'It sounds to me like there's something on your mind, old man.'

During the standoff that followed, Jessie curled into the folds of her tattered nightdress, groaning as the movement ignited another round of agony. Jethro glanced back and in that instant she saw Stone's hand move. She screamed a warning to Jethro but it was too late. As the sound of a gunshot quieted the chaos outside, his blood splashed her face and she managed a half-scream before he plummeted forward, landing with a loud snap and trapping her with his body. With her heart beating loud enough to wake the dead, she lay still, waiting as Stone barred the door then ran to the window and peered out.

'Jessica-Rose, listen to me,' Jethro whispered, urgently.

His fingers touched her hair but she didn't flinch. He was in a worse way than she judging by the blood seeping through his shirt and warming her skin. His arm, trapped at an uncomfortable angle across her body dug into her stomach and she grimaced as he moved to press his face close to hers.

'I know you're afraid, and you've got no reason to trust me, but I need you to listen.' He shifted his weight against her, his hand moving away from her hair and brushing her skin as he slid it down her

103

body. 'My arm's busted and I can't reach my gun, but I'll do what I can to stop Stone. If you get a chance to run, take it. If you don't, do exactly as Stone tells you. Don't fight. Don't argue. Do what you have to do to stay alive. Do you understand me?'

She nodded despite her apprehension. 'I remember who you are now,' she said through a jaw swollen and tight with pain.

Tears welled in his eyes. 'Then you remember, when you were a very little girl, how your ma used to sing and you'd stand on your daddy's toes and dance?'

It was a vague image that had been buried deep for a long time. She couldn't remember any of the faces, but she recalled how happy she had been, how safe the hands holding hers had made her feel as she swirled around a room filled with warmth and laughter.

She managed to nod.

'You're pretty like your mother,' he said, between raspy breaths, 'but you need my strength now.' He looked past her, towards the sound of footfalls thundering towards them. 'Don't give up, Jessica-Rose. Whatever happens, I'll find you. I owe Marianne that much.'

Just then, Stone's boot caught Jethro in the chest and, as he rolled onto his back, he grabbed Stone's boot and twisted, throwing him off balance. Jessie didn't wait around to see the outcome. As Stone careered away, she scrambled to her hands and knees, coming to her feet and breaking into a stilted run with the grunts and thuds of the fight behind spurring her on despite the crippling pain of a potentially cracked rib. By the time she reached the barred door, she was doubled-over and holding her breath, the strength already draining from her quicker than beer from a holed barrel.

Glancing back, she saw Jethro down on his knees, his arm crippled at his side, his head hanging low and bloody. As she clawed weakly at the bar securing the door, she saw Stone's knee deal Jethro a vicious blow to the head that snapped him backwards and left him unconscious, probably dead, on the ground.

A smile split Stone's face as he turned on her. 'Come here you.' He crossed the distance between them in a few quick strides, grabbing her by the hair and ramming the half-lifted bar back onto its supports while he listened to the pounding coming from the other side. 'Sounds like the cavalry have arrived. I'm leaving now, like I promised I would, but the plan's changed. Oh, don't you worry, we're not finished yet. You're going with me.'

Somehow she found the energy to fight him, to scream and scratch and kick, but it was a token struggle. With the ease of a man lifting a sack of grain, Stone hauled her up and over his shoulder breaking into a run to God only knew where. And then they were climbing, and smoky air filled her lungs and a light rain cooled her skin. Colour and sound blended in a sickening mix as the world began to spin and each jolt pushed her closer to the edge of insanity. And then she was falling, clinging to Stone's shirt, her nails digging deep into his skin until they climbed again. Only this time, he dragged her off his shoulder, throwing her face down across his thighs, and she closed her eyes against the stamp of hoofs.

'Now the fun really starts,' he said, kicking his heels.

CHAPTER 12

'Just what do you boys think you're doing?' the sheriff asked, barging uninvited into Matt's room. 'Neither of you is in any shape for a manhunt and I'm forming a posse as we speak, so you just simmer down and let me do my job.'

Shoving his pants leg down inside his boot, Matt glanced at the sheriff, but clamped down on the accusation that lingered on his tongue like a bad taste. If it wasn't for the lawman, Stone might not have gotten away so cleanly as he had done. As it happened, the sheriff had insisted that all able hands stay on the bucket line, leaving only a couple of old-timers to check out the warehouse. By the time Matt came to, they were dragging Jethro out, and Stone had made an unhindered escape up over the rooftops and stolen a saddled horse that just happened to be tied out back of the jail.

That had been a couple of hours ago, during which time the doc had fixed up Jethro's busted arm and cleaned his wound. Matt had watched with interest as the red-haired Scot peeled away Jethro's shirt. The bullet had ripped through the flesh beneath his armpit, messy but not serious. Jethro hadn't said much, but Matt couldn't help thinking it was strange that a back shooter like Stone should near as damnit miss such a broad target. Pretty convenient. And now, despite having his broken arm trussed up in a sling and a swathe of bandages bulging under his shirt, he was leading the search to rescue Jessie and bring in his nephew to face a rope.

'Forget it, Sheriff,' Jethro said, fastening the thong on the left-handed holster someone had found for him. 'By the time you get that posse together, Stone will be long gone. If they do happen to come across him, he'll kill Jess just to get you off his trail. Her best hope is for Matt and me to catch up with him.'

'But I'm the law in these parts,' the lawman argued, puffing his narrow chest out to comical effect. 'If I let every man Jack take the law into his own hands, I'll—'

'Look, Sheriff, you do what you have to do . . .' Matt shrugged into a slicker, moving stiffly to help Jethro do likewise. 'Just don't expect us to sit around doing nothing in the meantime.'

Together, Matt and Jethro faced the lawman like an impenetrable wall. Daring him to argue.

He looked them up and down. 'Well, I think you're making a mistake going after him alone, but . . .' His eyes narrowed on Jethro for just an instant, mirroring the uncertainty that twisted Matt's guts, then he shrugged and stepped aside. 'I guess you know what you're doing, Lomew. The posse'll follow along in any case. Lou Manners was an important man in this town and I aim to catch the scum that killed him.'

'Understood,' Jethro mumbled. 'Just don't get in the way.'

Matt enjoyed the look of indignation that burned on the sheriff's cheeks. Somehow, it helped to ease the stiffness that was gradually bending him over and he found himself walking taller, matching Jethro stride for stride. But, for all his show of alliance, Matt couldn't fool himself. When all this was over, maybe even before, he would have to face Jethro along the barrel of a gun. Until then, he would tread carefully only because deep down in his gut he had the feeling that Jethro was more concerned than he cared to admit.

'So, have you got any idea where Stone's headed?' Matt asked, as they reached the street and started checking the gear on a couple of waiting horses.

'Yep.'

'Care to tell me?'

'Nope.'

With his patience suddenly worn thin, Matt grabbed Jethro's collar, pulling him down as he tried to step up into the saddle. He earned himself a piercing stare but with his injuries there was little Jethro could do, except mock him with a grin.

'I'm not playing games anymore, Jethro. If you lead me on a wild chase to nowhere, I'll shoot you dead and leave you for the buzzards. Are we clear about that?'

Jethro grinned. 'I wouldn't expect anything less. Now, are you finished? We've got a good three-hour ride ahead of us.'

Matt held on a while longer, wondering why he was placing trust in a man who had sworn to kill him. He still didn't trust Jethro, but when you stripped away his reputation there was something likeable about him. Still, his motives for finding Stone and Jessie before the posse could, weren't clear cut and that made him dangerous.

They rode out of town just as the sun cleared the horizon. Matt kept behind Jethro, content to let him lead, and make himself less of a target in the event of an ambush. Whatever other crazy notions Matt might have, one thing he was sure of: this trail could only lead to trouble.

Jessie woke with a start, groaning as she bounced painfully against a saddle horn. Still face down across Stone's thighs, all she could see was the horse's belly and the rocky ground that shifted crazily as all her senses kicked in. Feeling dizzy, she closed her eyes again, willing herself not to throw up as the scent of horseflesh mingled with the rancid odour of male sweat and God only knew what other bodily odours emanating from Stone. She tried to swallow, instead choking as her mouth filled with vomit that exploded against the horse's belly, splattering back into her hair and face and leaving a trail on the rocky ground.

'You're awake at last. Good.' Stone smacked her backside. 'I was starting to get lonely.'

He raked his spurs against the horse's flanks, causing the animal to pick up speed, thereby kicking up dust and tiny rocks. Jessie blinked rapidly, fighting back tears of despair and pain as tiny specks of dirt worked their way through her lashes and lodged painfully behind her already sore eyelids. Stone slapped her rump again, laughing loudly as she struggled to keep one hand over her face while struggling feebly to stop him with the other.

Still she refused to cry, forcing herself to think beyond the breathtaking pain in her side, the indignity of being face down across a man's thighs, and what would happen when they reached their destination. Instead, she tried to focus on Matt, remembering how he had saved her from Ethan Davies. How he would save her from that man's son. The only problem was, the last time she had seen him he was plummeting from a burning building. And Jethro had told Stone that Matt was crippled. Despite her tough intentions, she started to sob, and again she felt the weight of Stone's hand on her backside.

Don't touch me! she tried to scream, but it was a silent revolt. The swelling around her jaw wouldn't allow anything more than a pitiful whimper to escape. Suddenly, the injustice hit her with a stunning blow. She hadn't done anything to deserve this. Why should she give in to Stone and the despair his ill treatment had rained down on her? What was it Jethro had told her? That she looked like her mother but she had to have his strength; that he

111

would find her. She almost laughed at the absurdity of pinning her hopes on a man with a reputation far worse than Stone's. But he had also told her he was her father, and however much she wanted to disbelieve him, she knew it was true.

It all came back to her now. She had been about four years old the last time she'd seen him. Just before her mother died. He had sat at her mother's bedside, holding her hand until her time got small. Jessie remembered climbing into his lap as her beloved mother slipped away, how his low voice had soothed her as he told her of the beautiful place where her mother would wait for her. She had cried herself to sleep against his shoulder, feeling a double loss when she woke up and he was gone.

Now with the horse slowing, and Stone chuntering his plans to himself, she felt her strength returning.

Stone shoved her to the ground, laughing when her head cracked against a small boulder and wrenched a cry from her before she could contain it. She closed her lashes on the tears, refusing to give him the satisfaction of seeing her cry. When she opened them again, he was mounting a ladder that led to a platform and some sort of mine about thirty feet above the ground. A sign strung across the entrance warned any would-be claim jumpers to *Keep Out*. It didn't seem to bother Stone as he wrenched it down and slung it across the clearing.

For a minute, Jessie didn't register her opportunity as she held her breath waiting for him to emerge. Then like a flame to a fuse, the idea that she could escape, became a reality. Looking around she noted a rocky incline to the right and a thin stand of cottonwoods to the left. The horse stood a few paces away, chewing on a clump of dry grass. There was only one way in and out of the clearing, and she intended to take it.

Holding on tight to the pain in her side, she dragged herself across to the horse and pulled herself up using the fallen reins. With her gaze pinned firmly on the entrance, she circled slowly, putting the animal between herself and the mine. Still Stone failed to appear. Struggling against fatigue, but driven on by the need to escape, she tried unsuccessfully to scramble on board the docile animal.

Coming from inside the mineshaft, she heard the crunch of boots on loose dirt. 'Look what I found,' Stone said, holding up a filthy bottle of amber liquid as he emerged onto the platform.

She saw a look of surprise cross his face as he struggled to adjust from the darkness to the light. If she was going to escape, she had to try now. Startling the horse with a slap to the rump as hard as she could, she scurried backwards more quickly than she had thought possible, disappearing into the shadows of the cottonwoods.

Finding her feet, she faltered when the ground shifted unevenly, every lurch tearing a sob from her as she ran blindly away from the sound of running footsteps closing in behind her. She tasted blood as she bit down on her lip, warning herself to be quiet, but the sound of her laboured breathing seemed loud as the chug of a train.

And then she fell. Hard. The skin tearing from her hands and knees as she skidded through the undergrowth. Desperate and disorientated, she picked herself up, unsure which way to go in the semi-darkness. Before she could decide, a dark mass smashed into her, knocking the wind out of her as she landed flat on her back.

In a split second, Stone straddled her stomach, further cutting off her air as she tried to draw breath. 'Thought you could run from me, did you?' he shouted, spittle flecking her cheek. 'Well. . . .'

He raised his fist. Suddenly the pain and fear were too much for her to handle. He might kill her, but she wasn't going to die without a fight. Feeling around with her hand, she found a rock about the size of a big potato. With one final burst of energy, she swung it, hoping to hit him in the temple but only succeeding in striking him across his already bloody nose. Stone roared with pain, lashing out and adding to the beatings he had already inflicted on her.

CHAPTER 13

Doubts continued to nag at Matt. He was taking a chance throwing his lot in with Jethro but what choice did he have? Maybe if the sheriff had been more willing, Matt would have ridden with the posse, but he doubted any of them would work as hard to find Jessie and Stone as he and Jethro would. He only wished he knew what Jethro's motives were, aside from killing him sometime before it was all over.

Matt looked around at the terrain. They had left the town behind them more than two hours ago and now they were entering a narrow pass. Its steep jutting sides made it an ideal place for an ambush. In places it was barely wide enough for one man to ride through and fallen rocks made it treacherous underfoot for the horses to move at more than a walk. Again he wondered if Jethro had chosen this route for a reason other than as a short cut to wherever they were headed.

'You seem to be getting a mite nervous back there, Matt,' Jethro said over his shoulder. 'There's no need.'

'Easy for you to say.'

Jethro chuckled. 'I'm riding point. First shot's bound to get me. The best a shooter could hope for would be a ricochet taking you or your horse down in the confusion.'

'I'm glad you cleared that up for me. Considering those odds, you don't seem too concerned.'

'I ain't. Even if Stone was up there, he couldn't hit us. Outside the saloon, didn't you see how he squinted at you? Kid can't see more than thirty feet in front of him. Why else do you think he always shoots men in the back?'

Well, that answered at least one question, but Matt didn't know whether the news comforted him or added an extra chill to the shivers running down his spine. Or maybe his discomfort was more to do with the stiffness that had settled into his battered limbs which made every movement feel as though he was being wrenched apart at the seams.

'How much further?' he asked.

Silence greeted him, but, as the pass widened out, Jethro reined in his horse and stared off into the distance. Pulling up alongside, Matt sat in awe of the sudden contrast between the white-capped mountains offering a picturesque backdrop to the lush green valley below. Smoke drifted on the air from the chimneys of several buildings that constituted a small town nestled alongside a fast flowing creek.

'Beautiful, ain't it?' Jethro mumbled. 'I thought once maybe I'd settle here and raise a family.' He ended on a chuckle. 'Do you ever think that way, Matt?'

The usual denial sprang to mind but it didn't pass his lips. If Jethro was looking for a weakness, he wasn't going to give him one. Instead, he asked, 'What happened to change your mind?'

'My brother Ethan.'

Matt stiffened. He hadn't expected the showdown to come so soon.

Jethro sighed. 'He forced me to choose between the life I wanted and the life I thought I deserved.'

It was uncanny the way Jethro seemed to be able to read him, and Matt shifted uneasily in the saddle. Somehow, it sat oddly with Matt that a man like Jethro could ever have had dreams of a decent life. And not for the reasons he might have wanted to believe. But because in twenty years, if he lived through today, he could be just like Jethro.

'Tell me, Matt,' he said, slowing his horse to a near standstill, 'how do you come to know Jessica-Rose – I mean, Jessie?'

Matt felt the canyon walls press in on him. The question was one that would only reignite the tension between him and Jethro and Matt hesitated over his answer. Even if he was destined to die, he hoped to at least make sure Jessie was all right before he abandoned her to a life on her own.

'Your silence tells me you're still worried you'll give something away and let me have the advantage,' Jethro concluded. 'So let me tell you what I think, and maybe you'll tell me something I don't know.'

Matt doubted it would be much of a trade-off, but at least while Jethro was talking he wasn't shooting. 'Go ahead,' he said, with as much nonchalance as he could muster.

'Well . . . I'm guessing you were a troubled youngster. George Weekes liked to take miscreants under his wing, try and convert them to the right side of the law before it was too late. He must have liked you though, to have invited you into his home. That'll be where you met Jessie. How am I doing?'

'Not bad,' Matt conceded grudgingly, 'but it was Jessie who invited me in. Mr Weekes didn't have much say in it once I was through the door. Even though she was only ten years old, she could wind him around her little finger.' The memory made him smile. 'But this is your story.'

'Not really. I was just making conversation.'

Matt doubted Jethro's motives were that cut and dried but the older man kicked his heels and they travelled the next half-mile in silence. As Matt had expected, heads turned as they rode into town. Even in a remote community like this one it was doubtful they hadn't heard of Jethro Davies. Matt slowed his pace, distancing himself as they plodded between two lines of buildings that were not only solidly built of timber and stone but also clean and well-maintained. Even the folks wandering between the shade of one porch and another, were well turned out. It reminded Matt of some picture he had seen in a dime novel titled *The True West* and as far removed from anything he had seen, until now, as a flying train.

A dark-haired kid, about nine or ten years old, ran beside them, his face bright with excitement as he stared at Jethro. Suddenly, he sped ahead of them, disappearing inside a doorway. As they approached, the jailhouse came into view and a man in his late forties, wearing a wrinkled grey suit and a sheriff's badge, stepped out onto the sidewalk. Pushing his Derby hat back, he waited for them to draw level, catching Jethro's reins and drawing the horse to an easy stop.

Matt braced for trouble.

'Jethro Jesse Davies, I was wondering when you'd show up.' The sheriff nodded towards Matt. 'Who's your friend?'

'His name's Matt Lomew. Matt, this is my old friend Bill Gration.'

Old friend?

The sheriff looked Matt up and down, showing only a hint of interest. 'Any reason I should know you, Mr Lomew?'

Still pondering the knowledge that Jethro should be friends with a lawman, Matt shook his head.

'Then welcome to Weekesville, Mr Lomew.' The sheriff smiled and shifted his attention to Jethro. 'Have you got time for coffee? You look like you could do with some.'

'Sure, and maybe you could get Elmer over here.'

The sheriff turned and nodded towards the boy who lingered in the doorway behind him. The kid took one last look at Jethro sliding from his horse, then burst into a sprint back along the main street.

Matt watched him, wondering who Elmer was and why no one in the town seemed particularly bothered by their presence. Noticing an elderly lady standing outside the general store opposite, he touched his hat and nodded.

'Good day to you, son,' she called across. 'Will you and Jethro be staying long?'

'No, ma'am. We're just passing through.'

'Oh, shame.' She sounded genuinely disappointed. 'Well, you tell Jethro if he wants me to open the old place up, he only has to ask. I'm Mrs Standen, by the way. You take care now.'

A dozen questions filled his mind, but following Jethro's lead, Matt tied his reins to the hitch rail and followed him and the sheriff inside the jailhouse. As he shucked his slicker by the door, he noticed the layout was a basic affair. A single room with two cells running along the back wall, off to the side a curtained area with a narrow cot and a washstand, and in front of that stood a desk with a well-worn chair behind it and two equally worn straight-backed chairs facing it. Finally, there was a pot-bellied stove in the centre, where Jethro stood already nursing a cup of coffee.

The sheriff grinned as he handed a cup of the thick black brew to Matt. 'Hope you like your coffee strong, Mr Lomew. I have to drink it that way. It helps me stay awake. Being sheriff in paradise doesn't exactly keep me busy.'

Jethro chuckled as he eased himself into a chair. 'Hope you ain't complaining. You always did favour the easy life, Bill.'

'You got that right, Jethro.'

They both laughed.

'How are Tina and the kids?' Jethro asked.

'Oh, they're fine. I've got five kids now. Tina had twin girls last fall.'

'You're sure right about having too much time on your hands.'

Reaching into a drawer, the sheriff pulled out a wooden flask, shaking it near his ear before leaning across to add a generous measure of whiskey to all their cups. His gaze rested on Matt, taking in the Colt before he returned the flask to its home and reclined comfortably in his chair, rocking back as he crossed one ankle across a knee.

'Cheers,' he said, raising his cup.

They supped in silence for a few minutes. It gave Matt time to think, although the scene made no sense to him. In the company of Jethro Davies, the last place Matt would have expected to find himself was having a drink with a sheriff, unless there were bars between them. But here they were, and aside from a few lingering glances in Matt's direction, the sheriff seemed as relaxed as if he were attending church on a Sunday.

'So, this doesn't look like a social call. What brings you back to these parts, Jethro?' the lawman asked, as the silence lengthened.

Glancing in Matt's direction, Jethro seemed to wait for him to offer up the story. When he didn't, he said, 'You remember my nephew Stone? Ethan's boy?'

121

The sheriff's expression stiffened, his fingers tightening around the cup. Somehow, the tension seemed to ease some of Matt's anxiety about the easiness between the outlaw and the lawman.

'He killed a man over in Garner. There's a posse behind us, but Matt and me are aiming to catch up with him before they do.'

The lawman's eyes narrowed, some of the friendliness disappearing behind a deep frown. 'Did you have anything to do with it?' he asked, addressing Matt.

'No. He's no friend of Stone's. Matt and I tried to stop him. I got this for my trouble.' Jethro cradled his broken arm before hugging his waist. 'And Matt . . . well, he already had one of Stone's bullets in his back before he got singed.'

It was an unwelcome reminder of his injuries and Matt curled his fingers, feeling the sting beneath the light cotton gloves covering his blistered fingers. He gulped the last of his coffee, suddenly fired up by the slow pace of the conversation.

'There's something he hasn't told you, Sheriff. Stone took a young woman hostage.'

The sheriff's Adam's apple bobbed, his cheeks paling despite their rich tan. 'Sounds like he takes after his pa. Crazy dangerous. You got any idea where he's taking her?'

Jethro nodded. 'Same place Ethan took her mother . . . fourteen years ago.'

'Good Lord, no. You mean Marianne?' The sheriff's chair crashed into the cot as he came to his feet. 'I'll mount up and ride along with you.'

'No.' Jethro staggered to his feet, gripping the sheriff's arm before he could grab his coat from a hook on the wall. 'This time I don't want the law around.'

Matt didn't understand the look of comprehension that passed between them, but it didn't matter. He had set out knowing what the outcome would be. Either he or Jethro wouldn't be coming back alive. But whatever happened, he had to know Jessie would be all right.

'I think he should come along. Jessie might need someone she can trust when all this is over.'

'You aiming to pull out?' the sheriff asked.

Matt shook his head, letting his gaze linger on Jethro.

'Something you two ain't telling me?'

Matt waited for Jethro to fill the lawman in, but all he got was a mocking grin.

'Me and Jethro have some unfinished business.'

'And what might that be?'

'I'm the man who killed his brother Ethan. Ain't no other reason for him being here, except maybe to stop me doing the same to his nephew.'

The sheriff laughed, a full-bellied roar of amusement.

'I don't see how that's funny,' Matt said, his ire rising. 'Unless this isn't a real town and you aren't a real sheriff. Maybe right now, that nice old lady Mrs Standen is drawing a bead on me.'

This time, Jethro joined the sheriff in his amusement.

'You've got it all wrong, Mr Lomew. Jethro is a big part of this town, but as for you killing Ethan . . . I'd say you did him a favour.'

'Do you mind telling me how?'

The sheriff's blank expression showed real confusion. 'Why? Because you killed the man who killed his wife.'

CHAPTER 14

A gust of wind circled the office as the door opened then slammed behind them. 'Did someone call for a doctor?' The craggy-faced man who entered did a double take. 'Jethro Davies. It's been a while.' He dipped his shaggy grey head at the sling on Jethro's arm. 'Are you after a second opinion?'

'No, Elmer, it's broke and no doubt about it. I was wondering if you're up for a ride out to the old silver mine.'

The doctor shivered visibly. 'Any special reason?'

'Ethan's boy, Stone, is up there. He's got Jessica-Rose with him.'

'Jesus Christ!' Elmer actually staggered. 'Your Jessica-Rose?'

Matt watched with interest as Jethro nodded solemnly. He wondered if maybe his fiery fall had done more damage than he thought and right now he was back in Garner, running a fever and hallucinating about this whole thing. He took a deep steadying breath and closed his eyes against the madness. But when he opened them again, the same three faces stared back at him.

'Have you put it all together yet, Matt?' Jethro asked, with a glimmer of amusement momentarily replacing the mocking stare.

'I think I'm starting to. Marianne was your wife, who was murdered by Ethan. And my Jessie is your daughter?'

Jethro grinned. '*Your* Jessie? I can see when all this is over you and me are going to have to talk.' His expression sobered under Matt's solid wall of mistrust. 'I would have told you sooner, but I owed my little girl an explanation before I told you anything.'

The possessive reference to Jessie riled Matt more than he liked to admit. If any of what Jethro and the lawman had said was true, it would take a while for him to accept it. A few disjointed words couldn't undo the years of constant unrest that had dogged Matt's heels since he had killed Ethan Davies, and nothing either man could say was going to make him change his game plan.

'Ain't no point yacking about it now,' he said, hiding behind his gambler's mask of indifference. 'Are we going to finish this?'

Jethro got stiffly to his feet. 'Bill, Elmer – I'd be obliged if you'd follow along but keep out of it until the shooting's over.'

Bill Gration nodded. 'However you want to play it, Jethro.'

Jessie came awake fighting and sucking in great gasps of air as she slipped from a dreamless sleep and back into the waking nightmare. As she tossed off the last vestiges of grogginess, she realized that Stone's weight no longer pinned her, but her hands and feet were tied making anything more than a pathetic wriggle impossible. And without the shade of the cottonwoods, the sun slanting down forced her to close her eyes as quickly as she had opened them.

'Good, you're awake.'

She cringed at the sound of Stone's voice, but it sounded faraway and after several attempts she forced her eyelids part way open to see him standing bare-chested and wet with sweat, leaning on the handle of a pickaxe at the mouth of the mine. He reached for his canteen hung on a sharp rock near his ear and took a swig of water before wiping his hand across his face. Blood smeared his forehead as he disturbed the gash across his nose, but if it bothered him he didn't show any sign of it as he straightened up and rolled his shoulders a couple of times.

'It's nearly time,' he said, ducking out into the open to stand on the platform with her.

She pressed her lips together, not wanting to know what for as he crossed the narrow space between them like a predator closing in on its prey. Dropping to his haunches, he grabbed her by the back of the neck, dragging her into a precarious sitting position before forcing the canteen to her swollen lips. Despite her best intentions to resist, she gulped the cool liquid, feeling it ease the tightness in her throat before coursing through her like snake-oil tonic.

'That's it, you drink it all down,' Stone said.

Something about his gentle tone worried her and she gagged, managing to turn her face away from the sweet tasting water which then flowed down her chin and soaked into the remnants of her tattered nightdress. Its sudden coolness sent a shiver through her, adding to the feeling of foreboding that seemed to block out the sun's brightness and plunge her back into despair.

'It's not poisoned, if that's what you think.' He took a long swig before tossing the canteen away. 'I just want to make sure you can scream when you need to.'

Stone's eyes glinted with mischief as he looked her over. But instead of the ravaging she expected, he pressed her back down onto the creaking boards, sat back on his heels and looked high up beyond her.

'I know you're up there,' he shouted, his words echoing around them. 'It's a long time 'til nightfall. But hey, don't you worry about me. I've got plenty to keep me busy.'

He threw himself down on Jessie, forcing his lips against hers while his hands groped everywhere. Feebly, she struggled against him and the ropes but it was useless. When his mouth moved away from hers, she screamed.

'Good girl,' Stone said against her ear. 'Now the real fun starts.'

He pulled her with him as he got to his feet and headed back into the mine. The skin on her bare legs and buttocks burned white-hot as he dragged her cruelly across uneven ground and over jagged rocks. When he eventually tossed her like a rag doll into the back of the mine, she was glad of the semi-darkness to hide the tears that streamed freely down her cheeks.

'I won't . . .' She struggled to form the words through swollen lips. 'I won't scream again. No matter what you do to me, I won't call Matt to his death.'

Stone chuckled and slammed his fist against one of the thick wooden supports holding the roof of the mine in place. It shifted just a little, but enough that the roof gave up some of its structure. As tiny rocks and stones showered her head and legs, she almost choked as she sucked in on her terror, refusing to give him the satisfaction of playing along with his plan.

'You'll scream.' Stone nodded his belief. 'Right up until the point where the dust and dirt fill your mouth and nose until you can't catch a breath and then the rocks crush you as you're buried alive . . . just like your mother.'

He stared at her long and hard. His gaze seemed to bore down into the depths of her soul, tearing open old wounds and releasing a flood of memories as suffocating as the dirt and darkness. Feebly, Jessie tried not to recall the day her mother had died, but the events of that summer afternoon were suddenly as clear as the cloudless blue sky.

'You used to live here with your pa. My mother used to visit, to bake and to clean the cabin.'

'I used to love those cookies she made.'

Jessie's mouth watered. She could almost taste the cinnamon in them. Yet even that pleasant memory brought with it an unpleasant aftertaste.

'You hated to share.'

'She made them for me,' he said, spitefully.

Jessie clamped her mouth shut. There was little point arguing over cookies then or now and Stone's darkening mood seemed to hint at a more deep-rooted grievance. But what grudge could a ten-year-old boy have had towards a three-year-old girl?

'She should have been my ma,' he said, as if reading the question on her mind. 'That's what Pa wanted, but she told him she couldn't leave you and Uncle Jethro. Do you know what that did to him?'

Jessie shook her head.

'It broke him, made him crazy sick until he wouldn't eat, didn't sleep. I couldn't bear to see him like that.'

Jessie cringed. She remembered everything now as history prepared to repeat itself.

Matt and Jethro headed towards the mountains beyond the town. It was impossible to ride hard. Neither one of them was in any condition to be sitting a horse let alone travelling over a little-used road that was barely more than an overgrown track. A half-hour later, Matt began to doubt Jethro's sanity as, side by side, they approached what appeared to be a solid wall of rock. As if reading his mind, Jethro chuckled.

'This is it. Just beyond that crest the ground slopes away into a narrow valley carved out at the foot of the mountain.' He closed his eyes as if picturing the scene. 'There used to be a cabin next to a clear running stream, a small corral and a lean to for the horses. Off to the right there's a small stand of cottonwoods.'

Just then, they topped a small rise and, as if from nowhere, the scene appeared below them, a sight more ramshackle but no less beautiful than Jethro's description. A horse, still saddled, dipped its nose into the stream but nothing else stirred. The cabin had long since rotted and started its return to the earth, but despite the lack of cover, he couldn't see Stone or Jessie. With panic starting to rise within him, adding to the nausea that came and went in waves, he took a minute to get the lay of the land. Wide open on three sides and bathed in glorious sunshine, there was only one small detail Jethro had left out.

'How do we get down there without being seen?'

Jethro looked down the gentle slope, the only way into and out of the area. 'We wait until the sun goes down.'

Just then, the sound of a shotgun disturbed the serenity of the scene. Both men slid clumsily from their horses, falling flat to their stomachs before crawling across the ground to peer again over the rise and into the valley. Inside the natural curve of the mountain and about thirty feet above ground level, he made out what looked like the entrance to a mine with a narrow wooden platform fronting it. Allowing his gaze to slowly wander, he glimpsed a flash of red against the cold grey backdrop and located Stone, about ten feet to the right and fifteen feet below half hidden in another recess.

Another shot boomed in the silence.

'What the hell's he firing at?' Matt asked as he watched Stone reload.

'The mine above. He's trying to cave it in. Do you see Jessie anywhere?' Jethro asked, wiping across his eyes before squinting again at the scene.

'No. Maybe he dropped her off somewhere.'

'She's here.'

'What makes you so sure?' Matt asked, apprehension already churning his gut as the sun disappeared behind a cloud and a few tentative spots of rain hit his cheek.

'Because the apple doesn't fall far from the tree.' He rolled to his feet and yanked the Smith & Wesson from its holster.

Matt rolled onto his back, feeling sick to his stomach as he looked up helplessly at Jethro towering over him, gun in hand. 'You had me fooled there for a while, Jethro,' he said, wishing now that he had undone the thong on his holster when they dismounted. 'I just about bought that story your friend the sheriff fed me. I have to admit though, I thought you'd give me a fighting chance when it came down to it.'

Below them Stone fired off another shot. Jethro sighed. It was hard to read his expression with the sun dipping in and out behind the clouds, but it didn't matter. Matt didn't need to see Jethro's mocking smile to know the final showdown had arrived.

'You still don't get it, do you, Matt?'

Matt decided to try and buy some time. 'Why don't you explain it to me?'

'This was never about me killing you.'

'That's not the way it looks to me from down here.'

Jethro stared at the gun in his hand, then slipped it back in its holster. 'I came for Jessie. To do for her what I couldn't do for her mother: to save her from a madman.'

CHAPTER 15

Matt accepted Jethro's outstretched hand. 'You've got some explaining to do, but right now we need to get down there pretty damn quick. Have you got any ideas how we do that without getting ourselves killed?'

'Nope. The best I can come up with is we ride down that hill like our hair's on fire and hope Stone doesn't get in a lucky shot before we reach those cottonwoods.'

Matt frowned at the idea then looked back at the distance they would have to cover in the open: 200 yards maybe even more down an incline that would test the horses' footing even at a trot. Not to mention the skilled horsemanship that would be required to stay in the saddle, and neither he nor Jethro were in any condition for fancy riding.

'Are you sure Stone can't see more than thirty feet in front of him? He seems to be doing a good job of hitting that rock he's aiming at.'

'The rock ain't moving,' Jethro said, drily, putting his foot in a stirrup.

'Then it seems to me we don't have a choice.' Matt swung up into the saddle and dragged his Henry rifle from its boot, firing off a succession of shots. 'See you at the bottom.'

As Jethro had predicted, Stone's aim was poor, but the odd shot winged close enough to make Matt flatten in the saddle. For a short while, it looked like they might make it. They were almost to the cottonwoods when Matt heard Jethro's horse scream. He didn't have time to look back but he heard the animal crash to the ground and kicked his heels, urging his own mount forward and into the relative safety of the trees.

Falling more than sliding from the saddle, he threw himself down and looked around for Jethro. The horse was down on its side. Blood showed on its neck and shoulder and its flanks heaved as it struggled to stand. Jethro had been thrown clear and lay a few feet beyond in the tall grass. Not a sound or movement gave a clue as to whether he was alive or dead and without putting himself at risk, there was nothing Matt could do for him either way. With Stone's shotgun once again directed towards the mine, it appeared he at least was assuming the worst.

'Just you, me and Jessica-Rose now, Lomew,' Stone shouted, during a lull in the firing. 'Do you think you can get to the mine and climb that ladder, especially in your condition, before she's buried alive?'

Matt ignored the challenge and after deftly loading a fresh magazine into his Henry rifle, he slipped his .45 from its holster, checked the chambers and slid it home. Remembering the spare Colt tucked into the back of his pants, he repeated the process. Satisfied that he was as prepared as he could be, he limped his way through the cotton-woods towards the sound of Stone's voice.

'Have you figured out how you're going to get from those trees to the mine without me pumping you full of lead?'

As he half ran, half stumbled, Matt pictured the layout. Between him and the mine, a distance of maybe 150 feet, there was nothing but a narrow stream and the collapsed ruins of the cabin. From his vantage point, Stone couldn't fail to hit him if he made a run for it. Under the cover of a night sky Matt would rate his chances as good, but nightfall was hours away and with the mountain rumbling its dissent, Matt doubted he had that much time to make his move.

He flinched as a pellet nicked the tree where he was standing, spraying him with splintered bark. Angry at his own inability to come up with a plan, he shouted, 'Why are you doing this, Stone? Let Jessie go. It's me you want, isn't it?'

'Don't fool yourself, Lomew. This was never about you.'

Matt didn't really care what Stone's motives were but he noticed the firing stopped while Stone was talking and decided to buy himself and Jessie some time. 'Then why seek me out, threaten me, take my girl?'

Stone's laughter mocked him. 'Because you killed

my pa and when I found out from Judge Bamford that he'd made arrangements for you and George Weekes's granddaughter to disappear, I just guessed you'd lead me to her. I waited a long time to make Jethro pay for what he did to me and my pa. The Bible says an eye for an eye. Well, he took Marianne from us and now I'm going to take Jessica-Rose from him. The fact that I get to kill the man who killed my pa just makes the wait that much sweeter.'

'That story doesn't make a whole lot of sense to me. I thought you and Jethro were partners.'

'I played him. All the time he thought he was helping me look for my pa, when I was just sticking with him waiting for the day he'd lead me to Jessica-Rose. I never guessed his guilt would run so deep that he'd abandon her and treat me like his own son, but it did my heart good to see him suffer every day.'

An eerie silence followed, seeming to echo Matt's confusion and question Stone's sanity at the same time. Cautiously, Matt poked his head around the cottonwood, taking a few moments to locate the place where Stone was hiding. As he watched, he glimpsed Stone's arm as he took aim at the mountain again. When the shotgun was spent, he dropped back out of sight. Matt almost laughed. Stone was a stupid son-of-a-bitch if ever he had met one. On a hunch, he fired off a couple of shots, pulling them short of Stone's actual hiding place.

'Is that the best you can do, Mr Fancy Gunslinger?'

Matt levered off another couple of shots, grinning as a surge of renewed optimism flowed through him.

'A rifle ain't my weapon of choice. But if you want to step down here and face me man-to-man. . . .'

He let the invitation hang as he adjusted his stance, leaning his shoulder against the cottonwood for much needed support as he sighted along the barrel of the Winchester.

'Maybe later. I ain't finished my story yet.'

Shoved back into the mine where the roof had caved in years earlier, Jessie came slowly back to consciousness. Stone had made sure with another beating that she completely understood his hatred for her. Not that there was any room for doubt. She remembered everything now. How fourteen years earlier, she had wandered into this same place looking for cookies Stone said he had hidden here. Being only three or four years old, she hadn't understood the danger, but the darkness had quickly swallowed her, leaving her frightened and confused. When her childish whimpers had brought no help, she had screamed until she was hoarse.

But she wouldn't give him that satisfaction this time and she dragged herself firmly out of the past and into the present. Shifting her head to ease the ache in her jaw, she realized she was lying face down in a pool of her own blood. Her nose had stopped bleeding but it hurt like hell and when the firing stopped all she could hear was her breath rasping through her split and swollen lips. Maybe it was wishful thinking but she could swear the shots sounded different now and were coming from further away. *Matt.* It had to be. A light-headed euphoria overwhelmed her and despite the direness of her situation, she started to laugh as she blinked back tears of joy. Matt had come for her, just as she knew he would. But her excitement died as quickly as it had flared into life as one of Stone's shots shattered some more rock, loosening one of the timber supports and setting the mountain to rumbling again.

With the mouth of the mine already starting to buckle under his bombardment, chances were she would be buried alive before Matt could get to her, unless she could help in her own rescue. It was worth a try. Fighting past the dizziness that Stone's brutality had caused her, she wriggled towards the light. Although no more than fifteen feet away, it seemed to take forever as she inched herself over the debris and decay of the earlier cave-in, hoping above hope that the pick axe she had seen as Stone dragged her inside would still be there.

As she got closer to the entrance, Stone's voice floated towards her, muffled at first then clearer. She stopped to listen, almost grateful for the interruption as sweat poured into her eyes and mingled with the blood from her nose to form a metallic, salty sheen on her lips that made her want to throw up.

'Jethro destroyed my pa long before your bullet could finish him off. The day he rode into this valley and stole Marianne was the day Pa really died. We loved her, but once she met Jethro there was no room for us. She ripped out Pa's heart and abandoned us.'

'Is that why your pa killed her?'

Jessie's heart soared as she recognized Matt's voice. With renewed determination, she started inching towards the entrance again.

'He didn't kill her. Jessica-Rose and this mountain killed her.'

Jessie shuddered at Stone's twisted truth. He made it sound as though she had caused the mine to cave in, burying her and her mother under layers of dust and rock. Her head swam with the memory, the walls suddenly closing in on her, sucking the breath from her body and tearing a scream from her despite the promise to herself not to give Stone the satisfaction of hearing her fear.

She heard Matt shout her name, and Stone's laughter as another shot smashed into the mine, shattering another section of the wall and the rotting wooden support that held the roof in place. As the beam shifted, she buried her face in the dirt, expecting to be crushed under the weight of the mountain as it surged against its restraints. But the rumbling stopped and when she opened her eyes again she noticed the pick axe where Stone had thrown it, half buried under the dirt and debris.

Choking on dust as she breathed heavily, she swung her legs forward and hooked her foot around the handle. It wouldn't move and her frantic attempts only left her weaker and more breathless. She stopped to rest and think, trying to order her thoughts. She was close to her escape now, close to where Stone's shots were hitting. If she tried to reach the pick, Stone might see her but if she didn't. . . .

'I'll kill you, Stone, you bastard,' Matt shouted.

Another exchange of fire erupted and in a moment of madness, she dragged herself into the opening. With the mountain shifting around her, she still somehow realized that if she wanted to escape she would have to free her feet first. Shifting her weight onto her back, she raised her ankles onto the blade and started the slow process of chafing the ropes around her ankles, hoping all the time that the creaking beams keeping the mine in place would hold just a little longer.

CHAPTER 16

Matt's arms ached with the weight of the Henry as he waited for Stone to make his next mistake, but he refused to give in to his weakness, instead mentally picturing Stone emptying spent cartridges and reloading the shotgun. As if to thwart his patience, the rain had started again in earnest now and he blinked rapidly as it splashed his face. Just a few seconds more and. . . .

He pulled the trigger almost before he saw Stone's red shirt, wondering if intuition or blind luck was guiding his finger. Whichever it was, his aim was true as he levered the Henry and heard Stone squeal. He didn't wait to find out if Stone was badly injured or just winged and he was already to the stream before gunfire kicked up dirt at his feet. But there was no going back as he glimpsed Jessie on the platform outside the upper mine. Almost naked, with blood in her hair and her face bruised and battered, she looked more dead than alive, but she was moving.

His gaze shifted quickly to Stone to confirm what the sound of the report had already told him. Stone no longer had the shotgun and Matt's chances had improved greatly. Added to that, Stone was standing out in the open now, one arm hanging limp and bloody at his side, his six-gun in his other hand. Realizing the Henry was empty, Matt dropped it as he staggered through the stream and grabbed for his .45. He was within fifty feet of Stone now, but, as he zigzagged his way towards the mine, he couldn't get off a clean shot. Luckily, for him, neither could Stone as his shots rained harmlessly left and right.

Both guns clicked empty at the same time and Matt let sheer momentum carry him the last few feet, tackling Stone to the ground and landing several hard punches to his face before Stone could react. But, as Matt had suspected that first day outside the saloon, Stone was a natural brawler and despite his handicap he managed to throw Matt off easily. They both came up panting, a few feet separating them as they eyed each other warily and circled for an advantage.

'You don't look so big without that Colt in your hand,' Stone said, spitting blood. 'And I've been slapped harder by a two-bit whore than that. We can stand here and fight all day for all I care, listening to Jessica-Rose scream as the mine collapses and buries her alive.'

Matt didn't doubt that with his own injuries, both from the shooting in Silver Springs and the fall from the boarding-house, he was no match for Stone in a fist fight, even if his adversary was one-handed and losing blood. But he'd be damned if he would let

Stone know that.

'I'm ready any time you are. With or without a gun, I'm going to kill you one way or another for what you did to me in Silver Springs and for what you've done to Jessie.'

Stone laughed. 'Hell, I reckon I don't mind paying for my time with her. She sure did feel good under all that satin and lace . . . and she was a real wriggler too.'

Matt lunged, head down, driving Stone back across the clearing and into the stream. Together they went down in the water, a tangle of arms and legs, neither one of them gaining the upper hand as Matt punched air and flesh in equal amounts. Again Stone wrestled him off, managing somehow to throw him face down. Before Matt could scramble clear, Stone punched him in the back, compounding the injuries Matt had been trying to ignore.

'Looks like I win,' Stone said, with the glee of a child as he pressed his knee hard into Matt's spine and yanked the old Colt from the back of Matt's pants. 'Makes me almost glad you didn't die in Silver Springs. I'm going to enjoy making you watch as the mine crushes and suffocates Jessica-Rose, and then I'm going to kill you with your own gun.'

He grabbed Matt's hair by the roots and slammed his face down into the water, holding it there while Matt struggled, the effort quickly draining the remaining fight out of him. When he came up, he again glimpsed Jessie. She was outside the mine now, standing on the platform, but when Stone let go of Matt's hair and fired off a couple of shots, she staggered back inside ducking as the mountain bore down on its restraints, showering her with dust and debris.

'Not long now, Matt. I'd say a couple more minutes at the most before the mountain swallows her up.' He rapped him over the skull with the gun, hard enough to hurt like hell but not enough to knock him out.

'You miserable son-of-a-bitch,' Matt gasped, words the only recourse left to him now that his body had finally given in. 'I should have killed you that day outside the saloon.'

'Yep, you should have,' another voice agreed.

Matt managed to lift his head high enough to see Jethro standing not ten feet away. Ashen faced and frail, he looked as near to death as any man Matt had ever seen, but he held the Smith & Wesson with ease and authority.

'Jethro.' Stone seemed to choke on the name. 'I thought you were dead.'

'That's a mistake you keep making.' Jethro laughed. 'But then you always were as dumb as a stick.'

'And you were always a mean old bastard.'

Two shots rang out, so close together they could have been one. Matt's attention stayed on Jethro where he stood stock-still, smoke curling from the barrel of the Smith & Wesson. On a hunch, Matt tried rolling. The movement, although small, was enough to shift Stone's dead weight and his body splashed lifeless into the water. For a second, Matt

145

stopped to look into Stone's staring eyes. It reminded him of looking into Ethan Davies's years before, only this time he felt no remorse for the death of a madman.

'I believe you now, Jethro,' he said, struggling to his feet.

'Then trust me when I tell you that mine's about to give,' Jethro shouted.

He was already stumbling towards it and Matt caught up just as Jethro reached the ladder, shouting for Jessie to come out and climb down. But she didn't appear and when Jethro quieted, Matt added his voice to the plea.

'Jessie, come on. Stone's dead, it's safe to come out now,' he assured her.

Her face appeared seconds later over the edge of the platform.

'Climb down. It's all right.'

'I can't. I'm too scared.'

Matt shoved Jethro out of the way, fighting his weakness and stopping momentarily to wait for another bout of dizziness to pass before he started to climb. It was hard work and he stumbled over each rung, the old ladder groaning under his weight before he was more than a few feet above the ground. Whether he or the ladder would break first was an even bet. He looked down. Jethro was struggling to hold it steady with only one good arm. As he watched, Jethro awkwardly threw off the sling, slammed his body against the rungs and wrapped his broken limb around the ladder, gripping his useless wrist with his good hand.

'Hurry up,' Jethro shouted. 'I don't know how long I can do this for.'

Matt didn't need telling twice. With a fresh burst of determination, he continued his climb, aware that the mountain was angry now, larger rocks falling from its face as the supports inside the mine buckled. Somehow he reached the top, his relief mirrored by Jessie as she slipped her bound hands over his head and wrapped her arms around his neck.

Somehow, he managed to hang on as the ladder shifted and he fought to keep his footing.

'Hurry up,' Jethro shouted.

'Jessie, I'm going to get you down,' Matt said, sounding calmer than he felt. 'I want you to climb across onto my back.'

She didn't move and he recognized the same debilitating fear in her that he had seen the night Ethan Davies killed her grandpa.

'Please, Jessie, I won't let you fall.'

'You're not strong enough,' she said, trying to pull her hands back.

He didn't need reminding of the weakness gnawing away at his muscles and sapping what little strength remained in his battered body. If he thought about it, he wouldn't be able to come up with one good reason why he wasn't lying helpless and defeated in the stream. And yet, he couldn't let her see his doubts and that in itself provided him with some untapped source of strength.

'I'm all right, Jessie. Please, just do as I tell you.'

Still she didn't move as tears leaked down her bruised and swollen cheeks.

'Do this for me, Jessie, and I promise I'll never leave you again,' he said, in desperation. 'I'll hang up my gun, pack away my cards and settle down, anywhere you like. What do you say?'

The platform shuddered as the mine finally gave in to the pressure of the mountain, belching out dust and rock as it reclaimed the stolen space inside. Jessie flinched, the momentum of that small movement allowing Matt to grab her and drag her clear. Now with her arms choking him as she struggled to wrap her legs around him, he was unable to tell if it was the ladder or him swaying. As the platform started to shift, he wrapped his arms around the ladder, kicked his feet clear of the rungs and for the first time in six years, prayed.

The ladder fell away before they reached the bottom and without the support of the platform Jethro was unable to hold it. Matt tried to turn his body so that he hit the ground first but it was near impossible and he felt Jessie underneath him as they landed in the dirt. Then he felt hands on him and saw the flash of a knife blade. Without thinking, he swiped at it.

'Easy, I'm just going to cut the ropes.'

The pressure around his neck eased and he rolled away, sucking in deep breaths of air as he watched Jethro wrap his coat around Jessie's shoulders. It was difficult to say if the fall had done her any more damage than Stone's beating. *Damn it!* If Stone weren't already dead. . . .

'Is she all right?' he asked.

'She'll be fine, but I wouldn't try to move, if I were you,' Jethro said, glancing between Matt's face and leg.

Busy catching his breath and concerned for Jessie, he hadn't thought about himself. Vaguely, he recalled feeling a stabbing pain in his leg as they hit the ground. Now, as he stared disbelievingly at the bone protruding through his pants leg, it hit him like a sledgehammer. Suddenly, he felt light-headed and the scene around him disappeared behind a pulsating cloud of darkness as he finally succumbed to his injuries and retreated to a place where there was no past, no future and no pain.

CHAPTER 17

Sitting in a rocker on the front porch of a little yellow-painted house with a white picket fence, Matt could still hardly believe his luck. That he was alive was a miracle in itself, but the picture-book serenity of Weekesville only added an extra element of disbelief to that fact. With the sun coming up and a gentle breeze wafting his face, he should be feeling at peace, but despite everything that had happened, he still harboured doubts about his future.

Behind him, a door creaked on its hinges and he heard the light tap of footsteps before Jessie placed a tray on the table beside him and handed him a cup of coffee.

'Peaceful here, isn't it?' she said, putting a voice to his thoughts. 'The kind of place a man could settle and raise a family.'

Standing at his side, looking along the street and out towards the mountains, she sipped her coffee in silence. As usual, Matt's gaze fixed on her. She had lost weight in the three weeks since her ordeal. And he suspected she was having trouble sleeping. He had heard her pacing about her room on more than one occasion when his own nightmares had kept him awake. Outwardly, all that remained to remind him of her ordeal at Stone's hands were a few faint bruises and some light scars that would fade given time.

She turned to look at him. With the sun shining off her blonde hair, she looked lovely and fresh in her blue print dress and as she reached across to push a lock of hair back from his face, his nostrils flared to fully accept the gentle scent of lavender that always lingered around her.

'How are you feeling?' she asked, gently.

'My leg still hurts like hell but the doc says it's mending.' He chuckled. 'But I don't need to tell you that, do I?'

She had been at his side day and night for the first week after they brought him back to town. The doc had told him that she refused to even let him tend her wounds until she was sure that Matt was taken care of. Sometimes Matt thought he recalled hearing her voice reaching out to him through the pain that seemed to live inside him like the Devil himself. Other times he would feel her cool hands on his skin and smell the scent of lavender before drifting off again into the darkness. Now, each time the doctor visited, he could hear her demanding a detailed account of his progress.

He clasped her hand, holding it between his as his thoughts took an unexpected turn. Here in this picture-book town with her standing at his side, he almost believed that a drifter like him could have a second chance. All he needed to do was ask her one question, and he already knew the answer to that. But a wall of excuses still stood between them, even if it was starting to crumble.

'Where's Jethro?' he asked.

'He went down to the sheriff's office, but he said he'd be back for breakfast.' She shaded her eyes against the brightness and looked along Main Street. 'That's him now.'

She waved at the lone figure coming slowly towards them. Jethro had changed since they got back. He walked like a man at ease with himself and his surroundings, nodding politely to anyone who passed him by. With his hair cut short, his whiskers trimmed and wearing a dark suit over clean boots, he could have passed for just another local citizen. But the most noticeable change about him was the absence of the Smith & Wesson.

Closing the gate behind him, he swept off his low-crowned, narrow-brimmed hat and grinned as he stepped up onto the porch. 'Have you got a cup of coffee there for me, darlin'?'

Jessie picked up the pot from the tray and topped up the cup she had been drinking from before handing it to him. 'Have mine. I need to go inside and finish breakfast anyway.'

He smiled at her affectionately but she bowed her head, barely glancing at him before she scurried away. Matt saw the disappointment on Jethro's face. It would take a long time for her to fully accept him

as her father, but she was coming round slowly and
Jethro seemed content to wait. Leaning against the
porch rail, he concentrated on drinking his coffee.
Although the mistrust between them had been laid
to rest, Matt still found it hard to talk to a man who,
for whatever reason, had dogged his trail for six
years.

'What's on your mind, son?' Jethro asked,
throwing the dregs of his coffee down into the roses.

Matt stiffened. Even now, after everything they'd
been through together, it still unnerved him when
Jethro spoke to him like an old friend. He forced
himself to relax. After all, Jethro was the only man
who could lay to rest the questions that had been
keeping Matt awake at night.

'Mind if I ask you something?'

'Go ahead,' Jethro said.

'How come you gave all this up to follow the
outlaw trail?'

Jethro chuckled. 'I wondered when you'd get
round to asking me that. I've been giving it a lot of
thought myself and the straightforward answer is: I
never did. Somehow I just drifted away from it.'

'I'm not buying that. One thing I do know about
you is you're no fool.'

Jethro smiled at the compliment. 'I was a lot of
things after Marianne died. I went crazy for awhile,
started drinking. I blamed my brother Ethan for
what happened, although when I look back I can see
it was nobody's fault, just an accident.'

'That doesn't explain how you came to be one of

153

the most feared guns in five states.'

'When Ethan left town, he abandoned Stone. The kid was devastated. He was only ten years old at the time and he begged me to help him find his pa. I guess I felt partly to blame for everything that had happened. You see, Ethan found this place and Marianne. They were going to be married and he wanted me there to see it. When me and Marianne laid eyes on each other, it was like that part of me that had been missing just clicked into place, you know what I mean.'

Matt shrugged non-committally.

'She called off the wedding to Ethan and within a month we were married instead. Ethan never really held it against me, although I knew it must have hurt him. Anyway, we all settled in this valley. Ethan started mining for gold and I started work for Marianne's pa, George Weekes. He was an architect, laid out all the plans and built this town from the ground up, but I struggled with it. I'd been running wild since I was a kid. Me and Ethan had been in trouble since we first stole candy from Old Man McGregor's store in Stantonville. George, he tried to help me – you know what he was like, he believed there was good in every man.'

Matt remembered the first time he had met George Weekes. Jessie had dragged him into the house when he came to the Weekes's kitchen looking for a free meal. He had been fifteen, recently orphaned and on the road to nowhere. His clothes were at least a size too small and he hadn't eaten a hot meal in three days. The only work he had been offered was cleaning out spittoons at the local saloon. Already he had been shot at and beaten by a couple of drunken patrons. The money he had earned had not gone on food or clothing, but on a gun and two bullets, all he could afford.

'Can you read?' George Weekes asked, after Jessie told him Matt needed a job and insisted he be the one to give it.

'Some,' he said, knowing that signing his name wasn't much to be proud of.

Matt had looked to Jessie, nine years old and standing behind her grandfather's chair, all bright curls and a flashing smile. Even then she had believed in him as she bobbed her head and urged him on.

'Yes, sir,' he said, smartly.

Weekes sighed as if he had the weight of the world on his shoulders. 'Well, I believe everyone deserves a chance,' he said, winking at Jessie. 'There are two roads you can take, Matt. My road, where you work hard, keep out of trouble and accept the challenge to make something of your life, or. . . .'

Matt didn't need to remember where Weekes told him the second road would lead. He had been walking it for six long years.

Jethro cleared his throat. 'Anyway, after Marianne died there was nothing to keep me here.'

'Not even Jessie?'

'I couldn't look at her without seeing her mother. It hurt too much, so I told George I was going to help

155

Stone find Ethan and rode out, intending to come back. Problem was, the longer I stayed away, the harder it got. Once I was out in the open, trouble just seemed to find me. Mostly, it was Stone's doing. He had a big mouth and a bad attitude and I just tried to keep him out of trouble.' He sighed. 'We know how that turned out.'

Matt refused to think about Stone. 'Didn't you ever wonder about Jessie?'

'Every day, when I was sober, which wasn't often in the early days. Problem was, I earned myself a reputation and George didn't like that. When he moved away from here, he just seemed to disappear. At the time, I thought it was probably for the best. Marianne wouldn't have approved of the way I was living and I felt I owed it to her to let Jessie lead a normal life.'

Matt smarted at the similarities between them.

'What happened when you caught up with Ethan?'

'We never did. He was always one day ahead of us. One town away. Always within reach but never within sight. And then one day, we heard he was dead, killed by an unknown assailant. No suspects and no witnesses.'

Matt hadn't believed it was possible, but even after his death George Weekes had been looking out for him. Within a couple of hours of shooting Ethan Davies, Matt and Jessie were on their way to Garner to start a new life.

'So why not come back then?'

'To what? Jessie was gone and Stone was out of

control. Ethan dying just made my guilt worse. I thought I owed it to him to try and straighten Stone out, but ... call it payback.' He stood up and straightened the sling on his arm as Jessie shouted to them from the house. 'If you're wondering whether I'd do things differently if I had my time over again, sure I would. Hell, I've got a lot of ground to make up but I've already started by unbuckling my gun and opening this house up again.' He looked at Matt with that strange piercing stare. 'You can do it, too. It's not too late for you. You've got a girl there who'll walk beside you, no matter what, but unless you can put the past behind you you'll never know what that means.'

It was the truth, but it didn't make Jethro's advice any easier to take. Trouble had been dogging Matt's heels for so many years, he still expected Stone or someone like him to show up and force him into a fight.

'I'm no good. She deserves someone who can keep her safe and make her happy.'

'And you don't?' Jethro slapped his hat against his thigh. 'Son, you're a fool. You risked your life for her, twice. As for a man who can make her happy ... speaking as a father and, I hope, as a friend, I think you're as likely to make her happy as any other man. I've seen the way you look at her with a twinkle in your eye. And I've seen the way she looks at you; the same way Marianne used to look at me. Stop listening for the echoes of a dead man. Accept that your fate and Jessie's are tied together and that pulling away will only tighten the knot and make you both miserable.'

Damn Jethro. He had a way of shooting from the hip, even without the Smith & Wesson, and hitting a man right where it mattered. And Matt couldn't disagree, but he'd be damned if he was going to let Jethro back him into a corner. He finished his coffee to the last drop, before placing his cup on the table and picking his crutch up off the floor. Jethro's fingers gripped his arm, pulling him up and holding him steady as he balanced on one leg and righted the crutch.

'I'm giving you my blessing,' Jethro said, walking away. 'Don't be a fool; just take it. It's not often a man gets a second chance in life.'

LIBRARY LINK ISSUES – For Staff Only

1	2	3	4	5	6	7	8	9
		326A						